Art of the Genre represents a huge shared world called *The Nameless Realms*, a place that spans thirteen extraordinary Ages of Man. Each category of fiction in this fantastic world has its own specialized medallion that is 'active' in the upper right corner of each book, thus allowing you to easily tell what specific genre you're purchasing. In the case of ***The Burning City***, you're about to enter the 5th age of Man, in a setting of Dark Fantasy, so the medallion you see above is the symbol for all books in that field.

THE BURNING CITY

SCOTT TAYLOR

Illustrated by
RK POST
JANET AULISIO
JOSH GODIN
and
JEFF LAUBENSTEIN

The Burning City
Copyright © 2012 Art of the Genre

Printed and bound in the United States of America 9 8 7 6 5 4 3 2 1

First edition: October 2012

ISBN: 978-0-9857674-4-0

This is a work of fiction. All characters, places and events portrayed in this publication are either fictitious or used fictitiously.

Cover: Gerald Brom
Interior Illustrations: RK Post, Janet Aulisio, Josh Godin, Jeff Laubenstein
Copy Editor Extreme: Joshua Villines
Graphic Design: Jeff Laubenstein
Book Design: John Woolley
Writing Instructor: Terri-Lynne DeFino
Sounding Board: John O'Neill

Art of the Genre
217 Palos Verdes Blvd,
#217 Redondo Beach,
CA 90277

artofthegenre.myshopify.com

Ordering Information:
For details, contact the publisher at the address above.

I'd like to dedicate this book to women who role-play. It's not an easy task sitting at a table with guys in what is most assuredly a male dominated hobby. Without you, the scope of what is acceptable and realistic to male gamers, concerning women, would be far more skewed in falsehood than it already is.

I also have to once again thank all the fans on Kickstarter who made this dream a reality with their generous donations. I know I say it everywhere, but it just never gets old. You are all the impetus that helped make the imagined a reality.

CONTENTS

FOREWORD ix

ACKNOWLEDGEMENTS..xi

PART ONE

    CHAPTER ONE.. 1

    CHAPTER TWO 9

    CHAPTER THREE 17

    CHAPTER FOUR 25

    CHAPTER FIVE 33

    CHAPTER SIX 45

    CHAPTER SEVEN.. 57

    CHAPTER EIGHT 69

    CHAPTER NINE... 79

    CHAPTER TEN 89

PART TWO

    CHAPTER ONE...101

    CHAPTER TWO 111

    CHAPTER THREE 117

    CHAPTER FOUR 125

    CHAPTER FIVE 131

    CHAPTER SIX 139

FOREWORD

The Burning City is not something to be taken lightly, and although I've written about war and death, there is certainly a stigma that can be attached to writing about sex, especially if, like me, you were raised in the very buckle of the 'Bible Belt' here in the U.S.

It's also difficult to portray sexual abuse, as it seems the epitome of a fall-back stereotype when writers decide to make a villain truly 'evil'. However, it is also a burden on reality to write a world in which sexual abuse doesn't exist since it has certainly been at the heart of human existence before the advent of the written word.

In this novel, it is my attempt to focus on sex as an act, one that simply happens, and the absolute distance it can actually have between the social conceptions of love and fidelity. I am in no way trying to convince readers that the acts involved in this book are justified or 'right', as your own values may vary widely, but that circumstances forced on people every day can form a shadowy side to what is an acceptable social perception when survival is on the line.

At its core, *The Burning City* is about life not always being what you thought it would be, crushing hardship, and a belief that men at their very core are sexually selfish.

Whatever your beliefs are on the subject, I hope you'll enjoy this work as much as we did making it. May your Element be ever strong, and you blade ever sharp! Long live the power and creativity of the small press!

Scott Taylor
August 2012

ACKNOWLEDGEMENTS

This is to acknowledge all the backers who helped make this book possible with their over-the-top donations. Thank you again!

Kai Nikulainen, Brandon Haase, R. Alexander Spoerer, Don Schlaich, Paul Weimer, Sean Murphy, Paul Woolman, Joseph Hoopman, Devin Harris, Ted Brown, Cody Markle, Gary Hoggatt , Ross Nicoll

Jay Kominek, TheJenPage, Jesse Sherman, Paul van Oven, Chris Thompson, Thom Walls

Aaron W, Grubnash, Michael Mock, Mike Tallon, Kenny Lynch, Peter M. Poulsen, April Steenburgh, Remy 'Rule-of-three' Hoffmann, Davrion, Mark Timm, Francis

Karl Hailperin, Norm Walsh, Justin Kowalski

Rhel, Matthew D. Wilson, Mikael Olofsson, Dani Akiyama, Peter aka Tyso the Pirate, Kelli 'Shay' Lind, Alex Torres, Vincent Ecuyer, Johnathan L Bingham, David Chamberlain

Brett 'Crasis Roma', Ralph 'Dula'

PART ONE

CHAPTER ONE

CAROLINE

Why do you wait there, just out of sight? Are you a ghost? Some spirit of the long-departed that lurks within these ancient halls from times when my father and his father before him hadn't dreamed of lands this far to the west?

I know not, and yet I feel you there, always watching, like an augur that something is about to happen I can't possibly anticipate.

For months I've wondered if perhaps you were a shade, a lurker sent by the Ebon Robe who now resides within these lofty towers at the bequest of the virgin Empress.

I think not, because spirits sent by necromancers shouldn't bring with them the thirst for knowledge that I feel from you.

My mother would say that you are a figment of my imagination, my father that you are a fallen avatar, a god trapped on this plane during the mighty closing after the Five Year War. I have to wonder, however, what my new husband would think, and yet I'm far too embarrassed and otherwise engaged to trouble him with such a question...

Caroline lay in the tangle of sheets, the smell of her groom's sweat mingling with the acrid smoke of the fire. She rested on her side, his arms around her as she nestled perfectly into the frame of his body.

The fire had become glowing embers, the wood burned down and the coals pulsing orange with the gentle breathing of the flue.

"Do you sleep?" Colin whispered.

A smile crossed her lovely face, and she replied, "No..."

His arms moved, pulled her over until she stared up at him in the shadowed light. The dim illumination of the fire was a kind mistress to his features, his tangle of copper hair subdued, his freckled cheeks smoothed clean, and the hauntingly pale shade of his green eyes cloaked.

He was not a handsome man, but man he was, near seven feet and broad as an ox at the chest, yet tonight he looked the part of any lovely Tiefon stage actor. Even his crocked smile was charming and serene.

"I've dreamed of this day for two years," he whispered.

She kissed him, "And I too, my love."

Without further preamble he rose atop her, arms like pillars on either side as she opened to him, her legs sliding out as his manhood found its way home once more.

Air escaped her lungs, his presence within more than she could accept. She ran a hand down his abdomen and held him partially at bay, even as each new thrust forced a subdued cry from her throat. The pain of it was harsh; each movement felt like someone was driving their fist into her stomach. His lips trailed down finding hers and she breathed him in, tasted his tongue and cried out as his pace quickened.

Banished gods... I never dreamed it would be like this.

A rogue tear trailed down the side of her face as he grunted, shook, and provided one more final impact. She kissed him again and then he fell away.

This was to be a pleasure... a gift... and yet I feel only a void at his leaving and a pain that lingers in both loins and mind.

"It's everything I could have imagined," he said.

She rolled over again, her eyes taking in the final gasps of the embers of the dying fire.

"And I too, my love," she repeated.

In moments, the sounds of his gentle slumber washed over her and she rose from the bed. Naked feet played on the cold floor, her course set to the water-closet as she squatted over a basin and brought an icy cloth to her tender lips.

She was swollen, and as she pulled the cloth away it was slick with a mix of blood and her husband's seed, the light of the Ghost Moon illuminating the potent smelling mixture.

Rinsing the cloth, she cleaned herself several more times before re-lieving her bladder and standing again. Her legs shook, and she gripped the marble top of the hand basin as she stared into the shadows of the silvered mirror on the wall.

Her hair was down, a long and tangled mass of dark curls, and the ashen stain around her eyes had bled back in lines to her ears with spent tears from her time amid the sheets.

You are a Lady... a Baroness born, and you will endure this just as everything else in your life.

Placing her hands in the bowl atop the chest, she brought cold water to her face and washed away the grime from her wedding night, the liquid burning her cheeks with each icy splash.

You love him, and he was your choice as much as your father's... what-ever is to be will come with more practice. The pain is temporary... it will get better... it has to get better.

She looked herself over again, tied her hair back, and then left the closet. Colin was snoring lightly in the large bed, and she slipped be-neath the covers next to him. He didn't stir, and she closed her eyes, sleep coming only slowly as the Ghost Moon was chased from the sky by its bloody sister.

Caroline walked the battlements of Inrest Castle, the mighty walls that stood vigil over the northern Gariny frontier. The lands around her had been reclaimed by her husband in the previous year, and her hand was his reward from her father, the Imperial Baron.

Spring bloomed among the thickets and forests to the south, a car-pet of green filling the newly tilled fields as the serfs worked to foster some living in the new province.

To the north, a vast plain stretched out, the land brown and the hills a sickly, mustard yellow that spread like a disease along the horizon. Wind from those climbs swept across the walls and tangled her hair, the smell like old ash and foul oil.

"If you're looking for a view, I'd suggest anywhere but the north," Nowin said.

Caroline turned. Nowin, her only friend amid the walls, had come up the steps to the Sister's Tower without a sound. She was small, just over five feet and kept her head shaved and polished. A single dragon tattoo trailed up her left shoulder to twist around her left ear.

"What brings a Wizard's wife to the battlements this day?" Caroline asked.

"I've free will, and with my husband away with yours this morning, I see no reason not to get some fresh air, be it tainted with the stink of the Ash Lands or no."

Caroline nodded and went back to staring north.

"Have you been watched again?" Nowin asked.

"Yes… I feel the eyes even now."

Nowin stepped forward, her hands moving along the parapet, a finger tracing a vein of metal in the stone.

"My husband says you sense powers beyond this world," she said.

"Gods?" Caroline asked.

"No… the gods are no more, the war saw to that, but there are other powers beyond this realm that even we cannot understand."

Caroline sighed, saying, "Perhaps, but I feel there's a reason the watchers have come, and I can't help but be drawn to this wall, my own eyes always seeking some answer in the north."

Nowin nodded, "If your answer lies in the north, then it is not one you should seek."

"Why? Am I not a Fleetwood now? Do not the bones of my husband's ancestors still reside in The Leopard Hills?" Caroline asked.

"There are no more Leopard Hills, only the Ash Lands and the Burning City at its heart serve as a marker to those fallen climbs."

"Which is the very reason my husband traveled half a world's width to come here. He seeks the truth," Caroline replied.

"The truth… that is a heavy burden to quest after, and I fear it will cost us all in the end," Nowin said.

Caroline smiled, "Fear not, Nowin of old Nextyaria, these walls are solid, and we have many a brave soldier as well as our fair amount of lofty heroes. Whatever darkness awaits in the north, it will not dare bring war against us or my father's growing realm."

Nowin nodded, but she did not reply, the wind growing in greater gusts and the smell of something alien trickling in with it.

Caroline woke with a start, her hand going to the empty space where Colin normally lay. A tremor shook the room, toppling a pitcher off a stand near the bed and shattering it on the floor.

"Zafin!" she called.

Her handmaiden didn't appear, and a subtle orange glow came from the windows at the front of the room.

Outside, a horn blew and men began shouting.

What trouble is this?

She got to her feet, drew her nightdress around her, and crept to the windows, the old panes distorting the view of the courtyard below. A signal fire burned on the battlements, black shapes sailing through the sky around it, the sound of combat rising from the court.

Behind her, the door burst open and Nowin appeared. She was dressed in a simple shift and carrying a spear and shield nearly as tall as she. The shield's face was emblazoned with a black dragon, and the edges of the defensive work were oddly angled and rounded in certain places.

"Nowin?" Caroline asked.

Nowin adjusted a spear in her left hand, shouting, "The keep is under siege. Put on an overcoat and boots. We've got to leave now!"

Caroline smiled at the joke, but Nowin's expression darkened before she spoke again, "This is no jest, and I'll not ask again. We may already be too late, and I'll not risk my life further, even for a friend."

She looked back at the court as something leapt atop a man, bringing him to the ground with a crash. A shiver went up her spine and she turned, raced to the chest at the foot of her bed and threw the latch. Well-folded clothes she discarded in a heap until she found a heavy cloak and hastily clasped it around her shoulders.

She drew the hood up, and raced to a wooden rack opposite the bed where her shoes were arranged in neat lines, a single pair of riding boots the only hearty pair among them. Grabbing the high-leather footwear, she pulled them on and turned back to Nowin who waved her forward with her spear.

"Come!"

She went, the two of them moving down a hall with Nowin leading the way. A scream echoed up through the stonework, and a sword clashing against something that wasn't steel rose from below.

"What are they?" Caroline asked.

"Insects, tainted things of the Ash Lands," Nowin said.

"But… those are just children's tales," she said.

"Tell that to the men dying outside."

They moved on, Nowin taking a servants' stair, a passage that Caroline didn't even know existed. It was dark, the only light dribbling down from the single-candle lanterns placed every ten feet in the arches above.

The stair grew thin, and Nowin turned her shield sideways as they twisted downward, a kitchen finally appearing in an orange glow from the great central oven.

A young girl in a scullery dress hid beneath a heavy wood table, her dirty face traced with tears.

Caroline took a step toward her but Nowin blocked the advance with her spear.

"We've no room for stragglers," she said.

Caroline drew herself up, nearly ten inches above the shield woman's height and taller still in her well-heeled boots.

"I am the Lady of Inrest, such decisions are mine to make," Caroline said.

Nowin's face was placid in the rummy glow, "There is no more Inrest, or haven't you noticed? You're the Lady of Death now, and unless you wish to join so many others, I'd forget your nobility and take my advice. I promise it's been hard won in more battles than you'd care to know."

Caroline looked back at the girl, and the maid pulled herself further beneath the table.

"Let's go," she whispered.

Nowin nodded and led them on, the door to the kitchen opening out into the common court, a late-season frost crunching beneath their feet as they fled across the yard to the wall beyond. Above, a man screamed and a splatter of blood steamed as it struck the ground near Caroline's feet. A sword tumbled after, the edge chipped and slick with more of the dark liquid.

She pressed her back further into the stone of the wall as a hissing came from above. Nowin readied both spear and shield.

"Whatever happens, stay behind me," Nowin said.

Above, the wooden walk groaned before a shape made the twenty-foot leap from the wall to the court. It was dark, covered in barbs, and vaguely resembled a black mantis.

Caroline drew in a breath, the thing's triangular head tilting at an impossible angle as it turned and regarded them. Behind it, along the wall of the keep proper, smaller shapes flowed over the vertical surface, their antennae waving.

"They're everywhere!" Caroline hissed.

Nowin took a step forward, runes alighting on the head of her spear. The creature raised twin arms, barbs at the ready, and the two clashed, spear slicing through its chitinous shell as black blood spilled over the frosty ground.

Another impact hit the walk above, and Caroline shivered, her breath coming in misty gasps. Nowin – her spear slicing the creature apart – drove it back before she ended it with a powerful lunge. The buzzing of wings cut her victory short.

Two flyers descended from the keep, and another dozen smaller, crawling things slithered off the wall toward her, their approach delayed a moment as two young grooms burst from the keep only to be pulled down as they ran.

Nowin turned, pierced one oncoming flyer, a bee-like thing, and deflected a second with her shield. The second creature broke away as another of the mantis beasts dropped from the walk above, this one charging Nowin without delay.

Caroline watched the crawlers pulling the grooms apart and then gasped as they moved on toward her, a cluster of them racing toward Nowin's back as she engaged the mantis.

By the banished gods… what horror has been brought upon this house?

Hands shaking, she pushed herself from the wall and took two steps to where the discarded sword rested. The bloodied grip stuck to her hand, and the weight of the thing made her grunt as she lifted it, but she brought it before her like Colin had tried to show her several times during their courtship.

Nowin deflected a second pass from the flyer, her spear blocking the mantis, but behind her the crawlers pounced, and she was overcome, a pile of the things washing over her as the spear and shield were consumed in their shadow.

Caroline screamed, causing the mantis to pause and turn. She had also caught the attention of the first of the crawlers, one close enough for her to smell.

Heat bloomed around her, the spark of her Human fire igniting as she brought the blade down on one of the smaller creatures. The insect was split in two by the weight of the blade. The strike tipped her forward, however, her motion and the shock of the impact ripping the sword from her fingers as she fell to a knee.

Before she could rise another crawler struck her in the back and she fell forward, sharp claws holding her, tearing through her heavy cloak.

A scream tore from her throat, more crawlers moving in as the one directly in front of her turned its back and lifted its wings. A stinking spray from its abdomen burst across her skin, the acrid odor slithering down her nose and numbing her tongue as the world spun and then went black.

CHAPTER TWO

COLIN

I am a Fleetwood, my father is a legend among that family tree, my uncle a villain, and my aunt the Empress of the World. This name is both my fate and my burden, and I have managed to carry it well even if my existence was a mistake, and no matter how many vows my father made to see the label of bastard undone.

In fair Lystbrook I was a king, an Imperial Baron, but that place was never my home and so I delivered it to the ancient Aspara keepers of the Wintertide and left to pursue another destiny. It was here, in the ancient and rugged climbs of Western Gariny that I found her, the woman for whom my heart was made to love.

Now, after two long years of service, she is mine, and I can think of little else but her. Me, a half-noble, a self-imposed exile, and man of lumbering ugliness, has been gifted a thing so beautiful my heart hurts for its luck.

That, is what I am, a man in love and it makes no difference if my surname be Fleetwood or any other...

Colin sat beside the fire, his eyes staring into the flame, his bearskin cloak drawn around his lightly-armored shoulders.

Beside him his less-than-lofty company was arrayed in the night. They were motley crew, but they were his, and with them he'd cleared

Inrest province of brigands, the unhallowed dead, and even the Ash Land insectiods that lurked in subterranean hives along the northern march.

"You look lost, Baron," Thorn said.

Colin broke his gaze from the flame and turned to the bowman. He was a hand taller than six feet, with long black hair that fell in curls and skin like the chocolate mixed with milk found in the noble markets of Nextyaria.

"I'm troubled, Thorn, but I've no reason to be so," he replied.

"Not true, my friend, you're missing her already, and there's no shame in that," Bara'Luur chimed in.

The dog-headed Lowl was nearly as tall as he, human-like eyes twinkling and the heat of his elemental spark tangible even above that of the camp fire.

"You were always one to understand passions," Thorn said to the Lowl.

Luur laughed, a lilting and broken cackle that which Colin found nonetheless unsettling.

"We Lowl must know such things, it is in our blood, same as the fire that resides with you Humans," Luur replied.

"And have Druids no passions then?" Dula asked.

"Druids are mingled blood, and even if I smell the wind on you, air cannot know the heat, but if given the chance it can fuel the flame and be warmed," Luur winked at her.

"Or consumed entirely," Roma added.

Luur cackled again, "What can a Wizard know of such things when water runs through your veins?"

"Are you saying a Wizard cannot love or know passion?" Roma asked.

"You tell me?" Luur countered.

Roma stared at the Lowl, the man's eyes dark and green and his hair black and touched in places with streaks of violet.

"I have a wife, does not that speak for something?" Roma asked.

Thorn shook his head and pointed a thumb at the Wizard, "This one... he always answers questions with more questions."

"Wives do not speak of love or passion, only a contract, the laws of nature driving such a bargain home to ensure the survival of the species," Dula began, "It is the trouble with Humans that they bring love and sex into the same bed, call it marriage, and inherently put their lives on the path to disaster."

"That's a comforting thought..." Thorn whispered.

Luur shook his head, "Whatever the case, Roma's wife is strange."

"In what way?" Roma asked.

"She has no spark… or none that I can smell. How do you explain this, Wizard, because I sometimes wonder if she's real or a construct, and if the latter, then what love can be found there?" Luur asked.

Roma fingered his staff, the supple black wood matching the darkness of his robe, before saying, "You should keep your nose from beneath my wife's skirts, Luur."

Heat blossomed from the far side of the fire as Luur showed his teeth and let a hand fall to the grip of his axe.

"Stop it, or I'll end this debate for good!" Colin hissed.

The camp was quiet, the heat fading as Luur finally broke eye contact with Roma before the Wizard smiled and placed his staff on the ground next to him.

"The Blood Moon is on the rise. We should sleep, the hunt tomorrow won't be long and then we can all return to our loves, be they real or imagined," Colin said.

He pulled the cloak around his shoulders and lay down, the sound of the crackling fire lulling him to sleep.

The company moved through the fields, sheaves of winter wheat golden around them, and the western horizon dark and threatening.

"What does the weather hold?" Colin asked.

Roma, his gold-runed hood pulled up over his head, replied, "The storm has passed west along the provincial skirts, it will not hinder us."

"I hate the rain," Luur grumbled.

The Lowl walked behind the Wizard, his chest covered in scale and plate, a sloped helm set between his pointed ears, and woodsman's single-bladed axe hefted across his shoulder.

Dula lingered in the rear, her cloak a supple thing the color of burnt mustard, and her dress like a patchwork of fall leaves that hid much of her slender form. She held mostly to her Aspara parentage, eyes blue and hair blonde and wavy, but her skin was drawn from the sea, pale and smooth, a gift from some water-born ancestor.

"I've no desire for rain either, but the keep isn't far, just a few hours and then we can find some peace," Thorn said.

"Peace, perhaps, but you'll be leaving soon after," Colin said.

Thorn smiled, saying, "Well, if you can't be away from your bride a full day, then how must I feel being a full season from my wife and newborn daughter?"

"I do appreciate the sacrifices you make, my friend," Colin said.

"They are not sacrifices when service is readily given, and I'd not feel right unless I saw to the final clearing of Inrest."

"Spoken like a true Academy graduate," Colin said.

"It's something we'll always have, so we might as well make use of those five years of teaching," Thorn replied.

Colin nodded, his eyes catching movement on the road further out among the fields. He watched it a time, the procession of dark shapes moving slowly toward the south.

"Caravan?" he asked.

"I smell blood..." Luur whispered.

"And fire," Roma added.

Quickening his pace, Colin pushed the party forward as Thorn drew his bow from his back while nocking an arrow. It was ten minutes before they made the road, and another five along it at a good speed, sweat trickling down from Colin's ginger curls before the first of the procession came into full view.

It was a single wagon drawn by three men in serf's dress, a straggling group of no more than two dozen following behind.

To the right of the wagon a man in chain walked, his tabard tattered and a spear half supporting him.

"Novis?" Colin called.

The soldier looked up, his face drawn, ashen, and covered in black blood beneath the left eye.

"Baron?" came the shocked reply.

Colin raced forward and the man swayed against his spear until he straightened and drew his fist across his chest.

"What is this?" Colin asked.

Beside them the wagon moved on, the hollow-eyed stragglers paying no attention to the company beside them.

"What's left, my Lord," Novis said.

Colin looked at the wagons and then back, "Left of what?"

"Of Inrest Keep, Lord."

There was a long pause, Roma breaking the silence. "Tell us what happened?"

Novis started shaking, his head moving back and forth but Roma slammed his staff into the ground and thunder cracked above.

Novis blinked, took a step back, and the wagon finally stopped as the serfs took notice.

"Speak!" Roma commanded.

The smell of the deep sea filled the area, the Wizard drawing himself up and the dark of his hair growing damp where it spilled out onto the front of his robes.

"Insectiods, Lord, they struck at the changing of the guard between the Ghost and Blood. There were hundreds… perhaps thousands, and the keep fell in minutes."

Colin shook his head, "No…"

"The Baroness?" Roma asked.

Novis whispered a prayer to the banished gods.

"This cannot be…" Colin's voice trailed off.

Thorn put a steadying hand on Colin's shoulder. "The keep is a big place, and Caroline is resourceful. This may not be the certain end a single, battle shocked, survivor makes it out to be."

Colin faced his friend, the man's handsome face and perfect skin such a contrast to his own. "You're right…we must move forward and seek the final truth."

He turned to Novis, pressed two hands to the man's shoulders. "Go to Otto Primus, tell the Imperial Baron that I've gone to find his daughter. If she is alive, I'll return her, if she's dead, she will be avenged. Do you understand?"

Novis nodded.

Sighing, Colin turned back to the company.

"Are you with me?"

They nodded, Luur giving a great howl as he raised his axe skyward. "Let us hunt!"

The road stretched out into the green thickets, and Colin began to jog, the greatsword across his shoulders creating a thumping rhythm with each step.

Inrest Keep loomed up like a charred skull atop a midden heap, a year's worth of labor and restoration having fallen away in a single night. The battlements were crumbled down, banners tattered, and everything consumable by fire lay in piles of grey ash that were steadily losing an unrelenting battle against the westerly wind.

Colin walked among the ruins, his legs leaden and his head hung low as he surveyed the carnage. The remains of what had once been men littered the main courtyard, horses lay in ruin, as did anything that once lived above ground in the keep.

Leaning down, he scooped up a plate amid the ash, the glaze chipped and bubbled over the surface.

I thought we were safe... what a fool I was!

"Colin!" Thorn called.

He rose, turned, and saw the bowman coming over the grey earth carrying a dress.

"What have you found?" he asked.

The man pulled up, his face stained black save for sweat that snaked clean rivers through it. He offered Colin the dress and he took it.

"It's the third I've found," Thorn said.

Colin ran his fingers over the fabric, some of it singed but no fire having truly touched it. There were tatters at several seems, and a rip along the chest, a bit of blood at the shoulder and another on a sleeve.

"What of it, I see nothing?" Colin said.

"I agree, but that's the problem. At first I thought it was a discarded spoil of war, but then I smelled it," Thorn said.

Colin brought the fabric to his nose, drew in a breath. Smoke filled his lungs, but beneath it there was a residue of sweat. He pulled it away, looked at it again.

"It's a scullery dress?"

"And freshly used, which means it's not seen a wash tub, and it was the same with the others," Thorn said.

Colin shook his head, "It's not uncommon for a dress to go unwashed."

"True, but all three? And don't forget the lack of blood, as well as the fact that no woman's body lay within dress like we've found with all the grooms, guards, and farmers," Thorn said.

Colin looked around, the charred and rent bodies of at least three men were all within ten feet of his position.

"There are no women..." he whispered.

Thorn nodded, saying, "They're gone, Colin, but that leaves hope, no?"

"Why? The Insectoids have no reason to take Human women," Colin observed softly.

Thorn shook his head, "I can't say, but at least we have something to go on."

From further off in the ruin a howl split the air. Both men turned and then ran over the crumbled stone and ash until they found Luur standing along the west wall, the Lowl perched on a boulder, his eyes facing north.

"What is it?" Colin asked, breathless.

A growl rumbled from Luur's throat before he answered, "I've got their scent. Caroline, Nowin, and others were taken here and driven north."

Colin followed the Lowl's gaze.

"The Ash Lands." Colin said.

"Revenge?" Thorn asked.

Roma approached, adding, "Revenge would mean they took Caroline, but all the women... no, something more sinister is afoot."

A shiver rippled down Colin's spine. He dropped the dress and spat upon the ground.

"Collect what you can, we're going north," he said.

"Colin..." Thorn said, his tone as soothing as possible.

He turned on his friend, heat pluming of him and his eyes dark, "I must do this, but I'll not ask you to come. You have a family, but mine travels north in the hands of evil and I'll not scurry south like some beaten dog."

Thorn nodded, looked north and sighed. "You'll need an archer with a good eye."

"And my nose to follow the trail," Luur added.

Roma walked away, as Dula stood silently by, her arms wrapped around her waist and her cloak drawn close over her shoulders.

Thorn looked after the Wizard, asking, "Will he come?"

"If Nowin lives, only the host of the Hells themselves could keep him from her," Colin answered.

"Dula?" Colin asked.

"I've been pressed into your service by my people, what choice do I have but to follow?" she asked in response.

"I free you of that service. You can return to the Wintertide if that is your wish," Colin said.

A wrinkle touched the corner of her mouth but she shook her head, "Then I will return, but only after I see your wife returned to you."

Colin sighed, "Then I will owe you much."

"No, we will be even, Human, and don't you forget that," she said.

Nodding, he turned back to Luur and Thorn. The two watched him, and he adjusted the sword on his back.

"There's no food in those lands, at least none that will sustain us, so whatever we can carry bring it, but remember that we must still be able to move with speed," he said.

The experienced warriors nodded and ran off, while the Baron stared north once more, the darkness of those lands like a cloak of night stretching away into the horizon.

Banished Gods...whatever happens just let her stay alive because I won't stop until I've found her!

CHAPTER THREE

CAROLINE

It wasn't supposed to be like this. I was supposed to take those vows with the man I loved, slip into some storybook bliss, and live happily ever after. My mother always told me a different story. That woman insisted that life wasn't so easy, that you had to struggle to appreciate what you truly had.

I thought my struggle would be in the bedchamber, but now I know what a fool I was. Yet, in all the horror of the last few hours you are still here, with me, watching, and I can't help but feel that is more a blessing than I first considered it.

If you are here, there must be a reason, a solution that I've yet to see in all this madness. At least that is what I can hope.

The wagons rolled steadily north, sun now blazing down on the caravan as it rumbled along. She was cast about the interior of her cage, every bump shaking her, pounding her, until she clung to the bars for support.

Unlike a carriage, these carts were drawn over rough ground by a collection of toiling insects, their spindly armored legs marching ever on until one would collapse and another would take its place, the pace of the march faster than any horse of the South.

Beside her Nowin sat with her naked back against the bars, each bump slamming her bald scalp into a bar until it bled steadily.

"You need to tend to that," Caroline said.

"What we face is my concern; a scalp wound just gives me focus," Nowin said.

Around them half a dozen other women, all naked, huddled in the cage and wept or stared hollow-eyed into the forever grey. Their transport was one of three drawn quickly into the wastes, a small army of insects chattering and buzzing around them.

"What do we face, then?" Caroline asked.

"You don't want to know."

"I demand to know," she said.

Nowin smiled, but didn't turn to her, "You still think you are the Lady of Inrest? Do you believe such demands mean anything in this cage?"

Caroline bit her lip, gulped back the tears.

"Colin will find me, and I will once again be the Lady, so I would well remember that," she said.

"Will he?" Nowin asked.

"Yes."

"And what exactly will he find I wonder?" Nowin trailed off.

Caroline shivered, whispering, "Your questions are tinged with darkness. It does not help…"

"Look around you, darkness is all we have."

Caroline looked back at the land, a blowing desert of ash and black sand swirling around their path.

"What of Roma?" she asked.

"What of him?"

"Won't he come for you?"

Nowin sighed, "We have a child, the boy residing in Nextyaria, that should be Roma's concern, and I fully expect him to remember that."

Caroline looked back at the small woman, age showing on her features and the dragon tattoo dark against her skin.

"Are you telling me to abandon hope?"

Turning, Nowin stared at her a long moment, then she smiled. The mirthful expression on the woman's face was so foreign that Caroline drew her arms up around her shoulders and shook.

"Caroline, I'm no oracle or fortune teller. I can't tell you what will happen in the future, or what our men in the South will do, but I want you to remember this," Nowin's eyes suddenly lost all laughter, and she looked intently into Caroline's, "I will be with you."

"What?" Caroline was surprised by the sudden change in the woman's tone.

Nowin reached out and took her hand, "I will be with you, and I ask you only one thing in return. No matter what happens, no matter how horrible our treatment, remember that I'm with you. Remember that we are one, and together we shall survive this."

Caroline shook her head, new tears coming freely, "I don't understand."

"This isn't about love, and it isn't about sex, husbands, expectations, or any other emotion. This is about two women making a pact that they will do whatever it takes to survive a world that is beyond all of your worst imaginings. Promise me," Nowin said.

The words caught in her throat, so Caroline nodded silently. Nowin took her hands, squeezed them until pain shot up her arms, and the smaller woman's gaze bored into her with such power she couldn't look away.

"Promise me, not from here," Nowin pointed first to Caroline's head, then her chest, "But here."

"I…"

"Promise and make it true. That is the only way," Nowin hissed.

A dam broke inside her, heat from her spark washing into the nothingness of Nowin's grasp.

"I promise," she said.

Nowin watched her another moment and then leaned back into the cage, her head bouncing and another spray of blood dripping down the bar.

"I'm going to hold you to that…" Nowin whispered.

Caroline nodded and then went back to staring at the glimmering darkness of the sands.

The camp wasn't alien, although it had the feel of a foreign nation, like one of the desert tribes Colin sometimes spoke of. Four dunes rose up around the settlement, a central well having been driven into the heart of the tent community, and a dozen metal boxes the size of a common inn's great-room bled back into the sand with leather tarps stretched over their tops.

Caroline was led to one such cage, Nowin and the others dragged behind her. To the left another cage rested. Its back was filled with part of the sheltering dune along with half a dozen shackled and bearded men resting beneath the shade.

The stink of the insects was fading, the army dispersing into the sands as the wagons were brought into the camp. Only the mantis captains remained, walking among tanned Humans and bronze-skinned Jai-Ruks. These new masters drove the women on, hands grabbing and eyes inspecting before the cage was slammed shut and a heavy lock thrown into place.

"The trial begins," Nowin observed ominously.

Caroline took a seat next to her on the sand, her bones tired from the abuse of the journey.

"What trial?" she asked.

"The purpose for our capture will be revealed here, and I'm certain you're going to find it the worst experience of your life," Nowin answered.

Caroline looked at the men and Ruks, a small collection of them talking in a foreign tongue close by. The Ruks were hard, grim creatures, dark-eyed and black-haired with a lower jaw that exposed two sharp incisors at their bottom lip.

"How do you know these things?" Caroline asked.

"If the insects had truly taken us, they'd have taken more than women, because food is their treasure. But we were stripped, caged, and transported which means a purpose born from the minds of men."

"Slavers?"

Nowin sighed, "Yes, but also men of the Ash Lands whose hearts could hold any number of darker purposes."

Caroline shivered, wrapped her arms around her breasts and drew back behind Nowin as one of the men broke from the company of his fellows and approached the cage.

He drew a scarf from his face, his chin covered in stubble and his face flat and wind-stained. Caroline tried to avoid his eyes, but he caught hers, smiled, and called out, "You, come forward."

She shook her head, and he frowned, a hand falling to a leather cord at his belt.

Beside her, Nowin hissed, "You made a promise."

Bile rose up in her throat, but she forced herself to stand, one of her hands moving from her breast to cover her loins. He waved her on, and she closed her eyes, whispered a prayer to outcast gods, and took several tentative steps.

"Ah, you're a fine one," he said.

Reaching through the bars, he grabbed her wrist and she gasped as he pulled her close. His breath smelled of anise, and heat connected with her own spark at the harsh touch. He turned her wrist and ran his rough hands over her palm.

"You're high born. No work ever touched these hands," he said.

"I demand to be released as my husband will pay whatever bounty you desire," she said.

He raised a thick black eyebrow.

"Your husband?"

"Yes, the Erg-Baron of Inrest, Colin Fleetwood," she said.

He smiled, looked over his shoulder and called in the same foreign tongue he'd use before. The group of men and Ruks turned, and one of the Ruks barked a guttural reply before he marched over to stand next to them.

The Ruk was tall, six and a half feet, with shoulders nearly four foot wide. He was muscled, well-kept, and wore a series of gold bands in his braided hair.

"She says she's a Fleetwood," the man said.

The Ruk looked her up and down.

"She doesn't look like one," he commented, with the perfect speech of a practiced tutor.

"Well, her husband is," the man said.

"What is your name?" the Ruk ordered.

"Caroline Sarise Hume Fleetwood," she replied.

"Who is your husband?"

"Erg-Baron Colin Fleetwood."

The Ruk nodded, turned and began walking away before he called over his shoulder, "Have her cleaned, bound, and taken to my tent."

The man laughed, and Caroline tried to pull away but he held her tight against the bars as he called for help.

Bracers shackled Caroline's wrists, their chains trailing up to a thick post driven into the sands. She knelt before it, naked and alone. Around her the trappings of a rich and well-travelled soul were arrayed. A low T'ungese writing table, a collection of Findalynn nautical lanterns, a Dravarian serving tray with full tea setting, and a bed of Aflyrian hardwood were just a few of the decorations that sat among heavy rugs and hangings of crimson and gold.

Incense burned close by in a brass urn, and a thick-headed dog lay near the door sleeping. Caroline's eyes were heavy, but the chains' promise of pain should she slump kept her from dozing off.

At a sound, the dog raised its head and so did the Baroness. The tent flap was cast aside as the Ruk came in. He pulled free of his scarf and carefully laid his coat on a stand. He still sported a shirt of mail with several long knives sheathed on a heavy belt beneath.

"I don't know what you plan, but this will win you no favor with the Empress," she said.

He walked to the tea setting, poured himself a cup, and then took a drink as his lower teeth clicked against the porcelain.

"The Empress?" he asked.

"Yes, the Imperial Empress, the World Mother, sovereign of every living thing that walks, flies, or swims."

He smiled, "You really think the Empress cares what happens to a distant relative who is not even of her blood?"

"My husband is her nephew," she said.

"Then perhaps she has some care for him, I cannot tell, but I promise you she, nor her agents, will ever know what has happened to you."

"Then you're a fool," she said.

He tipped his head, "Perhaps, but to this point my intellect has proved adequate, and the Ash Lands are not like other kingdoms in the World Empire. We have our own rules."

She pulled at the chains as he set down the cup, his heavy hands undoing the buckle of his belt. Her mouth went dry, and she pulled again, the spark inside flaring as her pulse quickened. Around her the smell of rich earth filled the tent, the Ruk pulling free of his heavy steel shirt.

"Human fire always amuses me," he said.

The chains clinked again as he moved behind her, his undershirt cast back on cushions to her right.

"This is your doom," she hissed.

Her voice broke as the words came out, and the smell of earth was so strong she found it hard to breath.

"Idle threats don't become you, Lady Fleetwood," he said.

His voice was close, and when his hand touched her naked hips she twisted and fought, her legs kicking out. She lost her balance, falling forward but the chains held her, and he grabbed one of her legs and pulled it aside.

"No" she wheezed.

Kicking again, she fought against his powerful hands, and her knees came back together but he reached up and grabbed a fistful of her hair. He pulled her head back, neck straining, and she let out a scream.

"I'll not give you a gift of earth in your womb. That blessing too good for you," he whispered in her ear.

He released her hair with a rough toss and got to his feet, her arms dangling from the chain as she fought against tears.

"There have been a thousand women or more who have passed through this camp and the others like it, all bound for the Burning City. Don't flatter yourself that I'd stain myself for the taste of your flame-kissed flesh," he said as he walked back to a low seat and fell heavily into it.

She looked up, a rogue tear betraying her as she spat onto the rug between them. He smiled, a slick orange shine running down his small tusks from the light of a nearby lamp.

"They say the Kin are the most powerful race of the elemental earth, but there are some among the Ruks who would dispute that fact. I am one of them," he continued.

Raising one of his black-nailed and gray-skinned hands, he turned his palm upward and closed his eyes. Around her the stink of earth rose from the ground like a palpable cloud and the fire within her guttered at the contact.

"I need not touch you to know you, to hound you, to make you mine," he laughed.

She struggled against her bonds, but the jangling of the chains mocked her, even the sound of them somehow deadened in the congealed air. Panic welled up inside as she felt the kiss of elemental contact on her naked skin. It was a though a thousand invisible serpents twined around her, their contact drowning her with their slithering touch.

A scream tore from her throat but was cut short as the taste of earth filled her mouth and she gagged. The scent, the clinging nature of the foreign element leached into her nose, circled and filled her ears, the defilement finding purchase in other places as she jerked and spasmed to prevent its intrusion. She lost track of time, of the screams, the tears, and the torment.

Inside, her spark flared, tried to fight, but the smothering might of the earth finally doused it to smoke and ruin. She sagged into the ground, knees buckling and the chains at her wrists holding her up as her eyes rolled back in her head.

Colin, I'm so sorry!

Darkness like the deepest night overwhelmed all as her spirit shuddered and clawed at her bones trying to stay against the perversion, but then, suddenly, the overwhelming power was removed. She gasped, bile rushing up from her belly as she vomited out the meager contents of her stomach. Her bladder released, the acrid tang of urine mingling with her regurgitation as she trembled and wept, a laugh rising from the low seat of the Ruk.

"You're not so noble now. Be thankful for this respite, the city will not be as pleasant a host as I," he said.

She hung there, half suspended by the chains, eyes staring into nothing until the Ruk called to some unseen servant and rough hands picked her up, unclasped the bands, and pulled her from the tent.

The camp passed around her, faces sometimes turning to meet her gaze, but in her mind they mingled in a kind of bright dream. Water was provided, hands washing her briefly before she was carried to the cage and dropped inside.

She lay for a moment, eyes watching the wind vibrate the tarp over her head until Nowin's face blocked the view.

"Caroline?" Nowin asked.

No words passed her lips. Nowin pulled her up, dragged her to the side of the cage and held her, the sun falling away in the west and the cool of the desert night creeping between the bars.

She shivered, eyes finally closing as Nowin whispered the same line over and over before sleep grasped her and pulled her into oblivion.

Do whatever it takes to survive... Do whatever it takes to survive... Do whatever it takes to survive... I promise...

CHAPTER FOUR

COLIN

She lives! I believe that in my heart. If I didn't could I even keep my feet moving forward, one heavy step at a time?

To what purpose she's been taken —revenge for my reclamation of old territory or some other dire purpose – I cannot say, but mark my words: I will find her. My comrades and I have seen many terrible things over the years, and we have triumphed over them one and all. This incursion behind enemy lines will be no different.

Even if I must take down the very foundations of heaven, then let it be so, for I swear by the Banished Gods, the very beings my family line drove from this world, that I've the will to take up the title of the Fleetwood name and bring a holocaust against any transgressor to my family!

The land was barren, a place of black sand, concealing dunes, deadly sinks, and cloudless skies that stretched on forever. Luur's nose kept them going ever on, the hours passing as they led a winding path among the wastes.

Colin carried a heavy pack, skins of water bound to its outside, and a long staff was clenched in his hand as he probed the sands with each step. He wore a scarf around his face, clouds of grey dust swirling around them as they walked and his eyes were covered with sand-shades, the tempered and blue-tinged glass keeping the blowing sand at bay.

"Camels would be nice," Thorn observed sardonically.

The man was walking next to the Baron, his head covered in a similar fashion and his staff working the path as well.

"Indeed, but the Keep was clear of them and they couldn't survive long in these lands anyway," Colin said.

"Well, at least it's not hot," Thorn added.

"It will be as the summer sun comes to these lands, but yes, a cold desert is much preferred to the scathing heat of those in the summer climbs of the world."

Ahead, Luur stopped along the rise of a dune, a low howl drifting back to the company. Colin looked up, the Lowl crouched along the lip and waved them up.

The company moved along the rise, sand shifting and sliding beneath their feet until they made the crest.

"What did you find?" Colin asked.

Luur pointed and Colin followed the scout's finger, a large shape appearing amid the tangle of three large dunes. It was a ship, a four-masted monster, tilted on its side with two huge rune-stone pylons extending from its port side, the starboard lost inside the sands.

"Skyship," Roma said.

"Why is it here?" Thorn asked.

"It's a Yanoan heavy bombard, probably come north to fight in the Battle at World's End, but when the gods were outcast, the deific magic that kept it in the air was lost and it came to rest here," Roma answered.

"Are you sure?" Thorn asked.

"I was there, and I saw many ships like this fall from the sky during the upheaval," Roma said.

Colin looked at the Wizard, his face young, not more than twenty-five years playing on his handsome face.

You were there with my father and yet you look younger than me. Truly a Wizard's water is long lasting...

"I want it," Luur said.

"What?" Colin and Thorn asked in unison.

"I want that ship," Luur answered.

"I'm afraid it's not going anywhere," Colin said.

"Perhaps, but it will move again, I've heard that the Yanoans are harnessing air elementals and binding them to the rune-stones. Ships are again taking to the skies of the world," Luur said.

"A mighty task, such a binding," Roma said.

Luur turned to the Wizard, asking, "Could you do it?"

Roman shook he head, "No, but she could."

They all looked at Dula, the Druid garbed in a her seasonal cloaks, the fabric having melded to the colors of the desert around her and the dress beneath now a shifting pattern of ashen sand.

"Such rituals are long and involved, and I have no reason to enact them for a Lowl's desire or a baron's order," she said.

"But you could?" Luur asked.

She looked at the ship, her blue eyes pale and touched with flecks of green.

"Yes, it is possible," she said.

Luur rumbled in his throat and nodded, saying, "Then I will make it worth your while."

"I doubt that. Money means nothing to me," she said.

"Who said anything about money?" Luur winked.

Colin shook his head, "This is getting us nowhere and certainly no closer to Caroline or Nowin. Let's be on."

"What of the ship?" Luur said.

"Luur is right, the ship might not be our purpose, but there could be something of value inside it," Roma said.

"Your wife is somewhere in these blasted lands and you want to go treasure seeking?" Colin asked.

"The Yanoans are incredible tacticians, map-makers, and cartographers, which means there is a good chance there might still be sky reviews of this land inside that vessel," Roma said.

Colin looked back at the ship, its faded paint still standing out against the darkness of the sand around it.

"You're sure this is the best option?" he asked.

"It is *an* option. If it's the best only the fates can know, but I'm willing to take the chance," Roma said.

"I'm with him," Luur added.

Shaking his head, Colin stood and then began descending the dune toward the ship, the company following his lead.

The rear of the vessel held an opening the size of a carriage, sand drifting into what might have once been an observation deck. There was no rail, however, and the old metal tethers rested in the overhanging ceiling.

"It's the eagle launch," Roma said.

The party looked at him expectantly until he continued, "Yanoan knights ride the birds, a ship this size carrying at least half a dozen of them."

"Well, at least they had a way home after the fall," Thorn said.

"Some of them, yes, but not all the crew," Roma corrected.

"The others would have had to walk out, and without Inrest reclaimed in the South that would have been a week-long or more proposition. It's not a pleasant thought," Colin said.

Luur sniffed, his nose exposed as he'd pulled his scarf down when they'd entered the dune's lull.

"Bugs," he growled.

Colin dropped his pack from his shoulders, Thorn following suit, as he pulled two gauntlet daggers from his belt and Thorn a gladius.

"Close quarters, not my favorite way to fight," Thorn said.

"Wait," Dula exclaimed.

Kneeling, she ran her fingers over the sand and whispered words. Beneath her touch the sands shifted, a creature appearing that was made of shifting sand. It bore some resemblance to a badger, and it shook itself, sand flying in all directions.

"I'll see if I can draw them out," she said.

Colin nodded, replaced his daggers and drew his two-hander from his back as Thorn strung his greatbow.

The creature moved forward, slipping into the interior as the party waited and the sun moved slowly westward. A dozen placid minutes later there was a rumble and the party stepped back, weapons at the ready as the sand-badger tumbled back out into the light, a black-mandibled head with a dozen eyes slithering out after it.

"Centipede!" Thorn yelled.

The thing rose up fifteen feet in the air, hissed, and venom dripped from its fanged maw. Thorn launched an arrow, the tip sinking deep into one of its eyes, and it jerked right and left as it tried to dislodge the shaft.

Two more of the things came from the darkness and the first low-crawler was met with Luur's axe, its head cloven off as the thirty-foot body spun and twisted in a coiling death throw.

"Wizard!" Colin called.

Three more of the things came out, the eagle's launch filling up with their shiny black bulk. Luur howled, his axe slicing another, but this one fell back and spat. The green spray missed Luur but hissed on the sand, steam rising. Colin stepped up and swung his sword, the blade's edge rending the arrow-wounded insect, innards spilling out as it fell onto the sand.

Thorn fired again, this time two shafts at once, and the face of the third centipede to emerge sprouted both barbs as he pulled back from an attempted bite at Luur's flank.

Behind the party, Roma raised his hand, his fingers brushing the air as he closed his eyes. The smell of the ocean, salty and wet, swept the dunes and the centipedes hissed. Light burst into existence in a single mote before him, the shimmer growing and tumbling forward until it swept into the thick of the creatures and burst into a cascade of lightning.

The insects shrieked and glowed, Colin and Luur stepping back as Thorn continued to fire at the writhing mass. Smoke rose, and the smell of cooked flesh swept away the scent of the sea, the half-dozen centipedes inside the launch falling to the sand as the cascade continued.

Roma kept his hand raised another half-minute until all movement ceased, then lowered it and leaned against his staff. His shoulders were stained with water, his hair slick and liquid dripped from his chin.

"This is not my domain, a desert is no place for a water-born, remember that before you call on me again," Roma warned.

Colin nodded, sheathed his blade and removed his daggers once more. Next to him Thorn unstrung his bow and Luur came forward to plant his axe into the head of a beast before he pulled a large hunting knife from his belt.

"Let's move in, and keep your eyes open, these might not be the last of them," Colin said.

"I'll stay with Roma," Dula said.

"Agreed, and watch the surrounding dunes, that display might have drawn other unwanted attention," he said.

The trio of warriors moved into the launch, boots crunching the cooked shells of the insects as they went.

"Now is when we need the Wizard," Thorn said.

They stood in the captain's cabin, the place a mass of charts, scrolls, books, and instruments. Some lay on the starboard wall, the listing of the ship having turned the room on its side, but the furniture was still held in place by brass bolts riveted to the floor.

Luur half-stood against the starboard wall, leaning down and picking through scrolls bunched there.

"I'm no chart follower. My nose leads me," the Lowl said.

"I thought you wanted this ship?" Thorn asked.

"I do, but I'll have to learn to use it, and once I do I'll invite others of my pack into the sky where we can travel the world seeking adventure."

"More like spoils of war." Thorn said. "Give it a year and the Empress will have the first sky raider on her hands."

Luur howled in agreement and went back to searching.

Colin picked up a leather-bound book and drew off the tether that held the covers. Light from a huge window at the front of the chamber was waning, the dusk coming fast and he squinted to see the words within.

"These are all written in Yanoan," he said.

"Go figure," Thorn replied.

Colin sighed, tucked the book into his belt-pouch and scanned the chamber once more.

"Found something," Thorn said.

The bowman drew a map from a shelf on the port wall, his feet wedged between a chair and a table to reach it.

"What?" Colin asked.

Thorn dropped a map down to Colin and he rolled it open, the face showing a grey waste played out on the surface.

"Well done," he said.

He moved to the starboard wall, found a clear spot and rolled the map out further, the light now so dim he had to draw very close to make out details.

"Where do you think we are?" Luur asked.

He ran a finger over the surface, the words were foreign but a portion of the southern side of the map had landmarks he could make out.

"That's the Lownmark River…" he said.

Luur pointed to another spot, "Then that's Inrest, although certainly changed in twenty-odd years."

Nodding, Colin ran his finger further north, "If I'm right, we'd be here." He drew a circle, his eyes going further north.

"What's that?" Luur asked.

The Lowl pointed to a circle of green fire at the map's center, three black towers rising from the flame.

"The Burning City," Colin said.

Luur ran his tongue over his dark nose, teeth showing, "I thought that was just a legend."

Colin sighed and shook his head, "No, it's very real."

Running his hand west, it ran past the grey wastes to a green land beyond and a single mountain that rose over a great blue lake.

"That's the Lupin Hills, and somewhere along those banks is your home, Thorn," he said.

The bowman drew close, his finger going out to point to a spot, "I'd say there."

"The Fleetwoods and the Lightlances were neighbors once, back at the close of the Fourth Age," his hand swept back to the wastes and the city at its center, "And this was all the Leopard Hills, the home of my forefathers."

"And the city?" Luur asked.

"Ka-Shu, The Barbarian Gate and capital of the land," he said.

"You Fleetwoods are too numerous, sitting the thrones of a dozen kingdoms from Nextyaria to Aflyr," Luur said.

"True, but this is where it all began."

"Until the God's Curse," Thorn said.

Luur growled, "Damn Arcxas and all his followers."

Thorn shook his head, "Well, I think you Fleetwoods got the last laugh in the end. The gods, Arcxas included, are no more."

"Perhaps, but the city remains, as does the curse that stole it from the world," Colin said.

He moved his finger down from the city, first marking a black settlement close to the flames and then another between their current position and the city.

"If this map proves true, and the sands haven't moved these settlements, then more than insects must live within reach of the city."

"And that might be the reason Caroline and Nowin were taken," Thorn added.

Colin nodded, folded the map and tucked it into the mail on his chest.

"Let's get back to the others, I don't want to be near this wreck when night comes," he said.

The trio moved back into the dark corridors, Luur lighting a lantern with a snap of his fingers, the heat and power of his spark twice that of his Human companions.

CHAPTER FIVE

CAROLINE

There are some things you can't return from. As I lay in the horror of what has become of my life I have to wonder if this is one of them.

Nowin is here, my only tether to sanity as I can't stop the pain that still lurks within me, the feel of the defilement, and the bile it brings to my throat. No revenge is enough, no tears enough of a potion to forget, and each time I close my eyes the visions come, my mind filled with the feeling of the earth upon me, in me, around me...

If this be my end, then take me soon for I have nothing left inside and will surely waste away and be blown to dust as I mingle with the darkness all around me.

Please... please... leave me here, let me go for I cannot take your eyes upon me any longer, be they sad or caring. It matters not. They are as invasive as that which has already been perpetrated on me and I can bare them no longer...

Caroline woke with a start, her own scream ripping her from a land of terrible dreams. Wind played around her, the grey sand covering her where she lay against the bars of her cage. The light was low, morning breaking the horizon in an amber glow.

"Nowin?" she whispered.

No answer. She lifted hers elf, looked about, those remaining in the cage a tangle of naked bodies around her. A shiver ran through her, the cold of the night having bled into her bones.

"Nowin?" she said again, this time louder.

"They took her," a voice said.

Caroline turned, the dirty face of a young woman staring at her from the bars of the cage next to her.

"She wanted you to know she would return," the woman said.

Caroline shook her head, "What?"

"They came for her in the night, while you slept, and she made me promise to give you that message."

Pulling her arms around herself, she rubbed the flesh from elbow to shoulder.

Now they've taken you, and I dread what is to become of your initiation.

"We leave this morning," the woman said.

Caroline didn't answer, didn't look to the other cage, but the woman continued, "Who took you?"

No answer.

"I guess it doesn't matter. In the end we are all changed, no?" the woman asked.

Somewhere in the camp a dog barked and along the front of the cage a giant mantis walked, its triangular head turning back and forth as the made its way out of her line of sight.

The woman resumed talking once the mantis had drifted into the morning gloom, "They say we'll be moving tomorrow, another step closer to the city and whatever final rest waits there. I once thought I'd live out my days in Lorin's Crossing, have Brutter the Woodcutter's children. At least until one drew the last life from me before I'd seen thirty winters. That is the fate of most women in my village. Now I see death is a gift, and all my prayers to avoid it have been cast back at me by some mocking demon."

Caroline remained silent but the woman continued undaunted.

"You talk different than the others here, and I've seen a lady once, passing on a carriage north for some special event in Ravenmoore. I'd guess if you're to go to the city, perhaps you'll be ransomed like the knights who are captured in battle while the common men are left for the crows."

"There will be no ransom," Caroline whispered.

"Have you no husband, no father who would pay these slavers with honeyed gold?"

"No, and why would either want me now after what has happened?"

"What, the sex?"

Caroline turned to the other cage, the woman staring back to her with a stupid smile.

"How can you smile? And besides, it was worse than sex…" Caroline said.

The young woman shrugged, "My first time was no different than what I've been delivered at the hands of these men. Why should I care about such things?"

Shaking her head, Caroline felt bile rise in her throat, "You're insane!"

"What did they do to you then?" the woman asked.

"It doesn't matter."

"Then why are you so upset?"

Caroline shook her head, "You have no idea what was done to me."

There was a long silence, then the woman said, "I'll not make light of it, nor judge it, but if you're resting here then it couldn't have been that bad."

Caroline's lip curled, "You know nothing!"

The women around them both stirred, and a dog barked again. She paid no attention to the other women, simply staring at the girl as her spark fluttered to life in her chest. It was the first time she'd felt it since her time with the Ruk. The morning had grown bright enough that she could make out more of her tormentor. The woman in the other cage was young, perhaps even less than her own eighteen winters, with hair of matted gold curls and a round face with a little nose that turned up slightly at the end.

"What is your name?" the girl asked.

"Caroline."

"I'm Torna, and I'm sorry if I upset you."

Caroline's shoulders slumped, a wave of nausea passing through her. "It matters not."

Torna reached through the bars, her fingers stretching toward Caroline. She watched the stained hand, the nails broken and sand hiding around the knuckles.

"I've never touched a Lady before, and if the city is to be my future, I'd like to know that at least I've done something no woman in my family ever has," Torna said.

Caroline's fingers twitched, but her hand slowly made its way between the bars until they touched those of the other woman. Their spark, both fiery, played along the contact and Caroline's heart eased.

"I heard the Lady Nowin whispering to you, and I repeated her words as well," Torna said.

"Do whatever it takes to survive..." Caroline echoed.

Torna nodded, "Those are good words, and I hope you don't mind if I use them?"

Caroline shook her head, "No."

Shapes appeared outside the cage and Caroline broke contact, the hands sliding back behind the bars. A chain rattled and the door was thrown open. The women in the cage drew back, all having been taken at least once before and their fire heating the interior as fear swept around them.

Three guards, faces covered in scarves, pushed Nowin inside, and Caroline felt her stomach jump. Her friend took a step, the door slamming behind her, and then stumbled. Caroline tried to stand but her legs had cramped.

Nowin recovered, stood again, and picked her way among the women until she slid down next to Caroline.

No words were exchanged as Caroline took hold of her and Nowin stared forward, eyes dark.

"Do whatever it takes to survive," Nowin hissed.

Caroline nodded, "I promise."

Behind them the door to the adjoining cage was opened, men yelling for it to be emptied. Caroline turned and looked back, Torna giving her a final wan smile before she rose and went with the others.

Above the sun crested the tents and dunes beyond, the heat of its kiss spreading over the cages and the women within.

Caroline lay against the bars of the cage, the sun boiling down on her back and the eyes of many of the women watching her.

This was not my doing.

Nowin sat beside her, the woman's bald head now covered in a fine brown fuzz, the dragon upon it fading from sight.

"Don't let the eyes disturb you, I'm here," Nowin said.

Her friend's voice was dry, and her right hand was swollen, a gift from one of her captors the third time she'd been removed from the cage. All the women had been taken multiple times, all but Caroline, and as the previous day wore on the mood in the cage had turned from shared misery to anger, the bulk of it directed at her. Their stoicism in the face of what she would have considered unimaginable abuse a week ago reminded the Baroness that the world outside the walls of the keep was far more brutal and harsh than a noblewoman could ever understand.

"I'll be fine," Caroline said.

Nowin turned to her, one of her eyes shaded violet and puffy, but she offered a thin smile.

"How is that?" Nowin asked.

"I've got to be… what other choice have I?"

Sighing, Nowin closed her eyes and leaned back. Outside, the wagon jostled along, a dozen drivers walking the sands around it.

"You'd do well to remember everything," Nowin said.

"What?"

"What has happened here, and what will happen next, will always be a part of you. I know you're building a wall now, and I don't blame you, but never seal it off completely because it will only grow if you do."

"I," Caroline trailed off

"I'm not saying you make it a cherished memory, but if you pretend it didn't happen, your life will become a lie that will eventually overwhelm you. If some kind of horror must befall us, take the only thing you can from it, a strength in the survival, and wait for your opportunity."

"Opportunity for what?" Caroline asked.

"Revenge, and let it be like nothing ever perpetrated before…"

Caroline stared at Nowin, the woman tranquil beside her with eyes closed and breathing steady.

What are you?

Caroline shook her head, protesting, "Colin will be the one..."

Nowin cut her off, "No, Colin is gone. Only you and I remain, so accept that and begin thinking for yourself. Stop pinning your hopes on what others will do for you."

Turning away, tears stung the corners of her eyes.

"I know this is harsh, but unless we look forward, we'll not be ready for what is coming. If Colin or Roma come for us, then that is a gift, but depending on it would be insanity. In life, there is only one sure thing you can depend on, and that is yourself. You can fail, but that is on you and you alone, and there is no one to blame in the end."

Outside, a driver whipped a Mountainback, the great beast pulling the wagon northward, and Caroline chewed her lip as she stared out into the dunes.

You will come, won't you? Do I believe Nowin's words or do I dream that you will save me?

The conversation trailed away, Caroline going quiet and Nowin falling asleep. Across from them a woman wept as the younger girl she held in her arms passed away, the blood trailing from between her legs dripping through the bars into the sand below. The part of Caroline that was still Human had the decency to feel shame that her first thought was for her own survival.

I will not be her. I cannot be her.

The sun, still at a tender angle in the early spring slipped west as night came on, only three days having passed since she slept in Inrest, and four away from her new husband.

Dunes grew deeper, and shadows longer in the waning light, a strange green glow rippling across the edges of the land. Caroline turned around, hands resting on the bars as she looked toward the head of the procession.

There, amid the sands, a tower stood, green as ghostlight and stretching into the violet sky until it bent at the top and drifted into the oncoming stars.

"Banished Gods," she whispered.

Beside her Nowin stirred. Her defender followed her gaze, the two of them taking in the monstrosity as it slowly grew with the passing of the hour. The night flowed in, and the glow grew, both of them shading their eyes against it.

"How big is it?" Caroline asked.

"We are still many miles from its base, and from what I'm seeing it is larger than Otto Primus, perhaps even larger Tristra."

"But what is the light?" Caroline asked.

"The Burning,the curse of the Arcxus," Nowin said.

Caroline shook her head, as green fire began to drift down around them. The ghostly tendrils of light slithered along the sky and impacted among the sands with puffing hisses causing the men around the caravan to extend shades above their heads.

The Mountainback blew a mighty trumpet as one of the falling flames struck it amid the leather tarps hung across its back. The green fires slid away in a liquid-like spray.

Caroline drew close to Nowin, the woman's hand reaching out to clasp hers. There was no spark exchange, Nowin having no such power, but still the contact helped ease the dread.

Around them the dunes gave way, the glow washing so heavily over the wagons that it was like a second dawn. A camp rose up, this one several times larger than the one they'd left the day before.

Tents dominated the mass of the community, but several stone buildings stood as well, slate roofs glowing in places from fire strikes. The tents were poled with rune-stakes, the rain of ghost-fire warded away when it came close as bubbles of magic appeared and evaporated the fire before it touched the fabric.

They passed a collection of Lowl, the dog-men watching them with Human eyes, spears leaning against hairy shoulders. More Ruks walked among the men of the camp, and there were other things as well, heavy cloaked monstrosities that shambled among the throng.

"If there is a Hell, we've found it," a woman said behind them.

Caroline shivered, the caravan turning into the west of the camp and a large collection of cages resting amid heavy tarps there. From somewhere in the distance the repetitive sound of a hammer drifted into the glow, each strike making Caroline wince.

What doom awaits us, and what new horror must I overcome?

Caroline was naked, but no chains dangled from her wrists as she was taken inside a tent the size of the Inrest's rear court.

Nowin's words drifted in her mind, as did her promise, while the flaps inside the structure drew back to expose a warm entry that spoke of new tortures. Braziers burned with orange coals, incense sticks smoked, and the floor was a rich carpet of rungs.

Her guards, two towering Ruks, pushed her onward. Another flap opened beyond the entry, this one to a circular solar that was exposed to the night sky. Green light spilled down upon them, the blazing tower of flame looming over as though it might crash down at any moment. A divan sat to one side, rugs still splayed aplenty beneath her feet, and a many-corded brass hookah resided in the middle of the chamber. Six other flaps were drawn shut around the circle, and the Ruks pushed her toward one on the right.

They pulled it aside and she moved from the unnatural green glow into a more subdued lamplight, this one touched in violet and the smell of sweet plums made her mouth water.

A woman sat at a table in the rear of the room, a strange oily black cloak spilling out behind her shoulders and eyes that held the same green tinge as the light of the tower above. She waved the guards away, the Ruks leaving with a bow and Caroline standing immobile in the middle of the chamber.

"I'm told you are Human nobility," the woman said.

Her voice was sanguine, and it held an accent that was both foreign and soothing.

"Yes," Caroline replied.

"Is it true you are a Fleetwood?" she asked.

"Yes," Caroline said again.

A smile spread across the woman's face, tranquil and sweet. She stood, her body dripping with thin bands of gold that lay among delicate silk wrappings placed more as decoration than true covering.

She walked forward, the air filled with a scent that made Caroline's mouth water and her palms sweat, the spark inside igniting.

The is wrong! I shouldn't be feeling such desires but she has a magic at work...

"Of what house does your bloodline run?" the woman asked.

"I have no Fleetwood blood, only that of my husband," she answered.

"Who is your husband?"

"Erg-Baron Colin Fleetwood, the former Imperial Baron of Lyst-book."

"Erik's son?"

Caroline nodded, "One of them, yes."

"Does he know you're here?"

"By now, yes, and he will come for me."

The woman's smile grew, her lips shining in the light. Caroline felt her knees weaken at the almost hypnotic magnetism of the strange woman.

Foreign desire rips through my mind and I want to kiss her, feel those lips on mine.

"Are you certain of this?" the woman asked.

Caroline nodded and the woman laughed, the cloak trailing out behind her rising until it flared out into a pair of silken black wings.

"You are more of a gift than you know, dear one, and I thank you for coming to me," the woman said.

Caroline's hand trembled and she reached out to touch the wings but the woman caught her hand. There was no spark exchange, only the empty contact much like the touch of Nowin.

"Only I say when someone can touch me, Human, and you will not be that soul this night," the woman said.

Nodding, Caroline drew here hand back, rubbing at the strange numbness that had settled into her fingers. Her mind swam in a mist of passions, confusion, and anger, but she could find purchase with none of them to help her focus.

"I know just where to send you, however, and because you have given me a gift I will return one to you," the woman said.

She walked back to the table, running long-nailed fingers over the surface before opening a lid in the top. A green glow spilled forth, and she drew out a crystal vial that sparkled with a golden hue at the edges of the green.

Turning back, she raised the vial to her eyes and looked inside, saying, "This elixir has no name, although many curses have been uttered concerning it. Yet to those that enter the city, it brings the blessing of life where only death would normally await."

Walking back across the carpeted floor, the woman handed the vial to Caroline and she took it, the crystal hard beneath her fingers.

"That is not my gift, as all who enter must have this potion, but I wanted to give it to you personally because I want to witness your soul," the woman said.

"My soul?" Caroline asked.

The smile continued, so warm and inviting it made her heart flutter in her breast.

"Yes, you see, if you take that potion it will change you. The greatest of those changes is that it will dry your womb forever," the woman said.

Caroline dropped the vial as though it was a viper, but the woman was faster still, her delicate hand striking out to snatch the crystal holder from the air.

Smiling still she held it out once more, "Waste not the gift I offer, for it means life where only death awaits, this I promise. If your Fleetwood baron is truly coming for you, it would be a shame to perish before he arrives, which surely you will unless you take this into you."

Caroline stared at it, her head shaking.

"No!"

"Does he love you or what you may give him? Who is his true love, you or a child that has the chance to steal your life even as you give it one of its own? There are no more Gods, and no priests and prayers to stay the hand of death that waits a woman in the throws of her labor, not like the time of your mother and the countless years before.

"Ask yourself, what is more important here, and what would he want?" the woman finished.

Colin, what am I to do?

"You hang to the notions of a backward world in which parameters are placed on things without true place or definition. Humanity ascribes meaning to the belief's in ideals and ideas contrary to nature. Once you break free of those shackles, accept that the body and the mind are two separate entities and free will is a curse, not a blessing, you can then begin to live. Hope is a dream and dreaming is for fools and weaklings.

"But you are still too young, too cursed with entitlement to believe my words for only suffering in the reality of live can make one understand. I promise you this, however, wisdom is knowing when to bow and when to stand tall, this moment, however, is certainly one of the former if you value life."

The woman's glowing eyes regarded her, the vial matching the tone of those soulless orbs.

Inside the tangled corridors of her mind the words of Nowin and the promise came back to her. Closing her eyes, she took the vial, drew off the stopper and brought it to her lips. The laughter of the woman slammed into her even as the liquid splashed over her tongue and burned on the way down.

"Yes... yes!" the woman laughed, "Drink deep of the gifts of the Burning City that you may enter and find all its other gifts just as tenuous and just as life-changing."

Tears fell down Caroline's cheeks, and her breath came in short bursts as she fell to her knees and clutched her stomach.

"You are ready, and so I will see you delivered. Then I will wait for my gift in return," the woman said.

Caroline shook her head, bile running to her throat as the guards returned, rough hands grabbing her up and dragging her from the chamber.

CHAPTER SIX

COLIN

I'd never dreamed of going this far into the Wastes, although it was always at the back of my mind to reclaim the fabled city of my fore-fathers. Such are the musings of youth, and life has a way of step-ping forward and showing you just how foolish such lofty goals are.

In two years I cleared the borderlands of Western Gariny. Along the northern march of the Ash Lands it was a vile territory and the cost in lives beyond my reckoning. The dangers of the place, even those remotely associated with it, were not for mortal men. Yet I persisted, I overcame, and even still I looked north and shuddered at what must lay over the grey horizon.

Now I am in it, a day deep and the power of our Wizard wanes as the dry climbs sap his connection to his element. What will be-come of this journey I cannot say, but I will continue on as I made a vow unbreakable. My life for that of my wife, and whatever trial I must overcome, then so shall it be, even if it means walking to the gates of the islands of Hell themselves.

A storm had blown across the grey wastes, the tail of it sweeping away west as the company drew out of the cloaked shelter which Dula had summoned. They each groaned and muttered as they stretched their legs.

"That has cost us time," Roma said.

Colin looked north, the sky scrubbed clear and the dunes shifted into a kind of valley around them.

"Two hours, maybe three remain to us," Thorn said.

A curse dribbled from Colin's lips, but he shouldered his pack and began a march up the nearest dune, the others following his lead.

When they topped the rise Luur drew close, his nose covered in sand along the bridge as he sniffed the air.

"She's gone... my friend, the scent lost to the elements," Luur said.

"Then it's a fine thing we have a map," Colin replied.

Moving on, his boots slid in the flowing sand as the sun crept ever west in the wake of the storm and each dune drew more and more strength from them. They stayed atop the ridges as best they could, but the northerly trek required trips into the troughs. This stole time and the light, and as Thorn helped Roma crest another such obstacle, Colin paused and took a long pull from his waterskin.

Beside him Luur knelt, the hairs on the back of his sloped neck rising. A growl rumbled from his throat.

"What is it?" Colin asked.

"A beast is about, and it stinks of scales and brimstone," Luur whispered.

Colin drew his greatsword as he turned back to the others now joining him along the ridge.

"Great Serpent!" he hissed.

Dula waved a hand against the breeze, her blue eyes flaring as she whispered prayers. Roma leaned against his staff, lips chapped and eyes sunken, but he nodded.

"What is your wish?" the Wizard asked.

"Stay here, and Thorn you stay with him," Colin said.

They both nodded.

"Dula, what can you provide?" Colin asked.

"I can ward you from its fire, but little else other than distractions," she answered.

"Do it," he said.

She wove her hands in the air, the wind picking up and her cloaks whipping around her. He smelled lilacs and tasted salt, his skin taking on the sheen of slate. Luur's hair turned grey and his eyes black as he stood next to him. Colin nodded before the two of them raced along the dune, the Lowl leading the way.

They crossed an arch of sand, one great dune marching into the next before Luur pulled up. Colin looked back, Dula having disappeared and Thorn and Roma black shapes in the fading light.

Luur pointed. A dune across the trough had a distinct curved abrasion in the otherwise virgin sand.

"It's gone around the bend and now persists beyond our sight," Luur said.

"If it belly crawls it's not winged," Colin said.

"No, sand serpents don't get their wings until they become elders, sometime around a millennia, and so few make it that far they are the rarest of any type of wyrm."

"Fire?" Colin asked.

Luur showed his teeth, "Yes, the worst trait of their ilk, but at least they have no venom."

Colin nodded, and Luur moved on, both men treading the lip of the dune until they came to a three-spoke part that led to connecting hills. Luur dropped and crawled forward, his face five feet from the junction lip when sand exploded and he rolled away howling.

The head of the serpent rose up fifteen feet above the dune's lip, two great fans at the back of its head standing out as a hiss reverberated down its body spilling sand from its tan scales in a cascade.

Colin drew back a step, his hands clutching the hilt of his blade as the wyrm's mouth opened and heat whelmed out. Fire licked at its lips, a spray of blue flames blasting down on the dune ridge.

Turning, the world around him became too blue, but only a heavy breeze touched his armor, skin, and clothing.

Blinking, he straightened up, a ring of glass now steaming white wisps around his feet as the serpent wove its mighty head back and forth in some strange dance.

Blessings to you Dula!

With a roar, he leapt toward the serpent, his boots shattering the glass beyond the ring. The beast drew back, its coils spilling out seventy feet behind it as he came forward and swung his blade.

The blow sailed clear, the serpent fast even for its size, but below Colin's position sand shifted and Luur broke low from around the base of another dune. The Lowl brought his axe against the thing's middle-scales and the edge bit deep.

The serpent hissed, twisted, turned and Colin charged again, this time his blade tracing a bloody path across the upper neck scales.

Another hiss spilled over the field, flames dancing from the creature's jaws, but Luur pressed the attack, his axe falling like that of a woodcutter. Blood splattered the sand after his second blow. The serpent snapped at Luur, but the Lowl rolled away and gave a great howl.

Boots sliding in the shifting sand, Colin closed with the serpent where its body rose from the ashen ground. His charge lacked speed, but he fueled the rush with a scream as he brought his blade down in a vertical strike along the underbelly.

Magic flared along the blade's edge, the scales tearing asunder and the pink meat within blooming like an opened sausage over a breakfast table. Blood spilled out and the great wyrm spun and twined, the coils wrapping the wound as it turned back to Colin.

He swung again, his sword ripping into the back of a coil and his arms shook as he connected with bone. A hiss above his head split the air, and the rear half of the serpent twitched and lay still, the weight of the thing's raised head pulling the whole to one side as it all tumbled down into the sand.

Luur howled again and charged to the beast's new resting place as fire bloomed into the sky. It turned its head, and Luur's axe bit deep into its jaw, several hand-sized teeth breaking away and tumbling to the sand below.

Colin set his feet and brought his sword down again, scales giving and blood splattering his arms as he continued to hack until the coil broke apart and the beast fell into two pieces. Beyond his position Luur continued to work on the head as the fire died and the mighty creature lay still amid the grey sands.

Arms trembling, Colin stepped back and fell into the dune with his eyes staring forward. He sat there a long time, the stink of the wyrm drifting over him and the sands dribbling down in tiny avalanches from where he sat.

Luur finally marched up to where he rested, ears forward and blood covering the better part of his scale shirt and bracers.

"That is a tale to tell," Luur said.

The Lowl gave a howl and Colin shook his head, saying, "If that isn't an ancient beast, I can't imagine what one would look like."

"True enough, but with Dula's elemental ward, we made quick enough work of it, no?" Luur commented proudly.

Colin shrugged, "Indeed, but that doesn't make it feel any less dangerous to be on these dunes."

"Think of Caroline, and you will remember that this danger is noth-ing," Luur said.

Colin looked up at the Lowl, brown fur swept back from the canine head that ended at the shoulder, the full body of a man residing below.

"You have a true warrior's spirit, my friend," Colin said.

Luur took a seat next to him, sands sliding them both down another two feet before they came to a final rest.

"What choice have I, as life is too short to waste on triviality and contemplation. We fire-born are not Aspara, our days numbered, and mine even more than yours," Luur said.

"The fire that burns twice as bright…" Colin began.

"…lasts half as long," Luur finished. "It's true, yet you have a century to live it, I perhaps three-quarters that, and the Eldaryn only half your number, but so is the blessing of fire."

"It is a short time," Colin said.

"What, do you want immortality? I see no blessing in such things, as life would become so trivial, so meaningless, that you would surely go mad with boredom or slip into a useless torpor, believing that most things are better left till tomorrow.

"No, I say live each moment as though it's the last, breathe in the life and expel great worth with each breath. That is a life to be lived, one worth living if you ask me. Without our drive this journey would not have happened, and the woman you love would fall away into memories of what once was instead of what can be."

Colin smiled, "When did you become the philosopher?"

"My mother was a hard Lowl, but she was also a teacher, and for that I've come to many a strange view, at least in the eyes of my people."

Above them, sand shifted down and the both turned to look up. Dula stood on the lip of the dune, her cloak blowing around her and dark hair spilling from within the cowl.

"An adult," she called down.

They looked at each other and then back at her.

"Please don't tell me we weren't supposed to kill it?" Colin asked.

Dula shook her head, "No, these are not beasts of the land. They are magical creatures and intelligent, thus they are not within the protec-tive domain of the Druids."

"Well, then your fire ward was an impressive gift as otherwise I'd have added my own ash to these damnable sands," Colin said.

She walked down the rise, her bare feet leaving a distinct trail from her passing.

"I'm glad my magic could aid you," she said.

"When has your magic ever not aided us?" Luur asked.

She smiled, a breeze kicking up around her, but didn't reply.

"We were just discussing immortality," Luur said.

Moving past them, she made her way to the serpent and ran her fingers over the scales.

"What of it?" she asked.

"That it must be a terrible bore," Luur said.

He drew his ears back and let out a small woof, the heat from him washing over Colin.

"Druids aren't immortal, so I guess I wouldn't know," she said.

"But you do have lives that are ageless compared to the likes of a simple Lowl," Luur said.

She moved further down the corpse, her finger playing along the scales until she stopped, pulled forth a small knife and worked a scale out of place.

"Yes, I suppose that's true, although Druids with Eldaryn blood would live far less than those with Aspara heritage," she answered.

"Like you," Colin added.

She slipped a scale into her cloaks and nodded, "Yes."

"Can we know?" Luur asked.

"Know what?"

"How long you've been alive?"

She turned, looked them both over, her blue eyes shining in the fading light of the afternoon.

"What solace would it bring?" she asked.

"None, perhaps, other than that of simply having an answer to a question which now will weight ever more heavily on our minds," Luur answered.

Nodding, she moved off toward the serpent's head, saying, "I'm nearing four centuries."

Colin turned to Luur who let out a howl. A smile, the first he'd displayed on the journey, crossed his lips and he got to his feet.

"Come, let's talk no more of life and death, I'm afraid of what the next revelation might be," Colin said.

Luur nodded, the two of them marching back up the dune as Thorn called from somewhere in the distance.

They awoke from their rest early, the Blood Moon still on the heights as they crept from their bedrolls and marched north. Colin's stomach churned and his muscles ached, the cool of the spring morning drawing mist from his mouth with each breath.

The grey sands stretched ever on, and Dula scouted now, Luur beside her as they travelled the dune ridges, the old map coming out from within the Lowl's cloaks on occasion until the sun rose gold and bright in the east and the temperature climbed steadily.

Sunlight cast long shadows in the troughs and Colin watched the inky shade as he drew off his cloak and hung it from the strap at his shoulder.

"The settlement should be close, look there," Thorn said.

Colin followed the man's outstretched finger, several plumes of dark smoke drifting into the sky along the horizon.

"They break their fast, and that means we've our chance at some revenge if we are quick about it," Thorn said.

"Nay, it is too far for a morning ambush, and we have no time to wait till the next morning," Colin replied.

Thorn nodded, and Luur came bounding along the dune ridge until he drew up short, saying, "I smell men on the breeze, and Ruks."

"There is a camp, we've seen the cook fires," Colin said.

Beside them, Roma drew close, his voice a rasping hiss and his eyes glazed, "If there is a permanent settlement, then that means there is a water source."

Colin nodded, saying, "Let's waste no more time, we will advance as though we're meant to be here, whatever people live in these wastes, they must respect strength, and that we have in abundance."

The march continued, weapons made ready and Dula spinning wind about her as she whispered elemental blessings.

An hour passed as they walked, the smoking towers slowly dying out and blown into the winds until only blue sky remained, but the smell of the camp drifted over the dunes and drove them on.

"Water... sweat... misery," Luur said. "It's all there on the wind."

"Let's hope they've dealt no misery to our women," Thorn said.

Colin's stomach churned and his palms were damp as the fires within kindled.

I do not enjoy death, but I will reap what was sown if it comes to that and no regret will linger in my memory.

A final crest fell away, a camp sprawling out amid an inlet among the sands, half a dozen hearty and broad-leafed trees sprouting around a ring of stone where open water lay. Around the cluster stood tents, more than two dozen, and in the leeward side of a sheltering dune a series of large cages lay tucked into the sand.

Roma stepped forward, his hand coming to rest on Colin's shoulder.

"Get me to the pool and magic will be yours for the taking," he whispered.

Nodding, Colin pulled the man forward, the company drifting around him as they moved toward the tents. Halfway down the last slope, dogs began barking and men and Ruks moved from within sheltering flaps, bright swords at their belts and scarves wrapped around their faces.

Colin kept his course, but a throng of defenders assembled before them as they passed the first ring of tents. Somewhere to rear of the camp a Mountainback blew, and Colin stopped short as a thick-shouldered Ruk drew a length of ugly black steel from his belt and stepped forward. The Ruk was tall, but Colin still towered over him like a giant before a troll.

"What brings strangers to the Bane Camp?" the Ruk asked.

His voice was that of a civic speaker but thick with the earth, and the smell of him was like that of newly tilled fields in the spring. The camp captain wore a shirt of bright mail, and a collection of wicked daggers hung from a thick leather belt at his waist.

"We've come seeking water and trade," Colin answered.

The Ruk, his face bronze and his golden eyes covered with long black hair that hung about his cheeks, waved the sword at each of them, "And what would any of you trade?"

"We have magic and coin, enough to gain slaves and a drink," Colin answered.

The Ruk laughed, as did several of those in the gang.

"Magic and coin? You're nothing but soft southerners, born in the womb of the mundane, and what do you know of magic? Certainly the coin we trade here has far more value than anything mined within the bowels of this world."

The Ruks and men around the leader nodded, fingers straining the leather on the hilts of weapons.

"Then you'll deny us water?" Colin asked.

"Who are you to ask for it?" the Ruk replied.

Colin turned his neck, twitched the shoulder on which his sword rested and then answered. "I'm Colin Fleetwood, and along with water, I've come for my wife."

The leader took a step back, eyes showing their whites for the briefest of moments, but Colin caught it.

Extending his leg, Colin rammed his boot into the lead Ruk and sent him into the others, his sword coming free of its sheath in the same action.

Thorn raised his bow, and arrow firing into another Ruk at the throat. The smell of earth and ash bloomed in the air.

"That one lives!" Colin screamed, with the tip of his blade pointing out to the Ruk he'd kicked. Blades were drawn around the area, and Dula raised her hand, palm up, and the sand burst into the air around them all.

Men and Ruks cursed, eyes blinded in the dust devil, and Colin swung his sword before him until it connected with a shadowed enemy.

There was a grunt, warm mist splashing his cheek, and he called back to his company but the wind stole his words.

A curse slipped his lips, and he stumbled over a body as he staggered forward. Only sand and shadows remained, but one drove forward, a metal blade striking out and connecting with the mail at his side.

The smaller blade ran across the metal scales with a shriek and pain pulsed in his ribs as he dropped his blade and grabbed the hand of the enemy. Their sparks collided. The swordsman was a Human, and Colin turned the man's wrist with a jerk. The short blade fell away, a cry of pain proceeding it, and Colin pulled him close as he brought the bracer from his left arm against his enemy's face.

The thick metal along his forearm connected with bone before the man fell limp in his grasp. He dropped him, drew daggers from his belt and marched on, his ribs aching with each step.

Where are you?

The sand was choking, coating his tongue but it faded as quickly as it came, grains falling from the air as the light of the day poured back among the tents of the camp.

Three bodies lay behind him, and Thorn and Luur moved back to back with blade and axe at the ready. The gang had dispersed, and he caught sight of fleeing robes among the tents. At the open well, Dula stood with Roma, the Wizard's back now straight and his cowl thrown back as water dripped from his hair.

"Luur, I need that lead Ruk!" Colin called.

Luur let out a howl and moved away from Thorn as he wiped a layer of sand from his snout. Turning away, Colin took one step before an arrow hissed and the head bit deep into the unarmored flesh at his thigh.

Two more shafts sailed clear, one so close to his cheek it cut strands of his copper hair. Wind spun up around him again as he fell back a step, the shimmer of the twisting air warding away a forth shaft.

Four bowmen lurked at the corners of tents to the west, and one of them pitched forward as one of Thorn's red-fletched shafts took him in the chest.

Another arrow was turned by the air wall, and from somewhere deep in the tents a thunderous roar broke over the camp.

"Roma!" Colin called.

He limped backward, a hand on the arrow in his thigh as blood dripped down his leg into his boot. Roma held his staff forward, the smell of the sea permeating the oasis as the Wizard drew forth his Afterglow. Suddenly three shapes, their visage like lions made of white light, leapt from the staff and loped away toward the remaining bowmen.

The enemy broke, but the lions were faster, horrible screams coming from behind tents a moment after they'd disappeared from his sight.

Beyond the screams, a tremor shook the sands, and then another as a black shape rose above the camp. It was vaguely Human, ebon-skinned, and misshapen with huge lengths of chain that hung from wrists the size of ale barrels.

"Formaian!" Colin called.

Roma continued his artistry and a flash of light broke the sky between the well and the creature, the blast splattering energy up the giant's chest and across its grotesque face. It bellowed, clawed at its cheeks and took steps toward them as a tent collapsed beneath its feet.

Firebirds burst into life amid the azure sky, their blazing wings dripping fire as they spun in a flock that circled the giant. The beast cried out again, the birds falling into it and exploding with white light at each impact.

Colin turned his attention to the east, as Luur and Thorn disappeared between two tents. He cursed, kept pressure on his leg and fell further back until Dula's hands stopped him.

"Be easy, that's no playful wound," she said.

Her hands guided him back to the well and the shelter of the trees, Roma standing at the edge of the green circle with staff raised and water dripping down his arms.

The Formaian was closer, his dark skin blotched with gray, and tent fabric and ropes trailing from his bowed legs.

"He draws near," Colin said.

Roma paid no attention, one hand waving like a man moving a brush across canvas, light shimmering and coalescing into a ballista before him.

Colin smiled, whispering, "Nice touch."

Dula drew out the arrow with a quick pull and pain erupted in Colin's mind as his eyes darkened.

"Banished Gods!" he hissed.

"Keep your eyes on the fight, it will distract you," Dula said.

"Assuming I don't pass out you mean," he replied.

"I've seen you take much worse, so stop being an infant," she said.

At the tree line the ballista fired, a shaft of pure energy blazing across the distance and finding purchase in the giant's chest. The towering beast staggered back a step, another howl erupting from its throat.

"It's been damned, cursed by some black art of earth. No normal giant could take such punishment," Roma said.

"Meaning?" Colin asked.

"Meaning it should be dead, and yet it moves on," Roma said.

Dula wove her hands over his leg, whispering a prayer before she drew out her side-satchel. The pain eased a bit, and the flow of blood stanched in the wound.

Another ballista bolt fired, his time taking the giant full in the face and part of its jaw tore away. Black blood spilled down its neck and chest, the essence of it touched with a haunting green glow.

"That's interesting," Roma observed, his tone that of an alchemist studying a new flower.

Colin shook his head, "Only you would think so." Turning, a drip of water hanging precariously from his chin, Roma provided him with a thin smile.

"It is interesting, the magic held in that thing's blood shouldn't be present in the world, at least not after the Great Closing and the Fall of the Gods," Roma said.

Colin hissed as Dula drew a bandage of spidersilk over his wound, saying, "You mean it's god-gifted?"

Roma shook his head, the ballista firing again, "No, but it's an Archipelago enchantment, some kind of necromantic integer or soul magic."

"You lost me at Archipelago," Colin said.

Dula chuckled and Colin looked at her, the ageless woman's wavy hair spilling down around her hands as she worked to bind his wound.

"Laughter from you? That's new," Colin said.

"I guess you Humans are finally rubbing off on me," she said.

Colin turned back to Roma, beyond the Wizard the giant now sat on the ground, blood pouring from its jaw and one shoulder ripped asunder.

"Can you explain your statement, but act like I'm not an Order apprentice?" Colin asked.

Roma flipped a finger, the ballista firing again, "It means someone here has access to otherworld magic, and unless there is a forgotten cache of the stuff, enough to waste on that behemoth, then a trade route beyond my understanding exists."

"You think it has to do with the City?" Colin asked.

"Why not ask him?" Thorn said.

A Ruk was cast into the line of trees, the earth-born's handsome face marked with the punishment of combat. Luur and Thorn stood over him, both of them holding blades slick with blood.

A resounding thump echoed from the camp, the trees swaying above as the giant finally succumbed to the Wizard's magic.

"I've come looking for my wife," Colin said. "And I believe you know her fate."

The Ruk showed his lower teeth, but a boot to the back of the head from Luur closed his mouth.

"I don't know what you're talking about," the Ruk hissed.

Colin nodded and waved Roma forward, the Wizard's black and gold robes swishing around him as he drew off his travelling cloak. The Ruk's eyes grew wide.

"You've heard of the Ebon Robes, yes?" Colin asked.

The Ruk nodded.

"Roma *will* have the information I require, so you have a choice. Tell me voluntarily or don't, but I promise you've not understood the meaning of pain until he begins his work," Colin said.

CHAPTER SEVEN

CAROLINE

So I've taken everything I've known, wanted, and prayed for my entire life and thrown it into the flames.

Wouldn't death be a better prospect? Was the way I chose, as noble as I'd like to make it, the coward's way?

If the demoness's words are true, I've given up my legacy in exchange for a future that is a curse on the husband I purport to love. But I do love him, I do!

Still, why would he love me now, after what has happened, the choices I've made, after the promises I've made? I'm damaged goods. The girl I was just a few days ago is no more, the pit of my stomach churning with bile and the dreams and aftershocks of my suffering coming in vile waves I can't turn back.

My skin crawls at the thought of a man's touch, and I know I cannot be anything like I was before. Deep down that might be why I accepted the vial, why I drank deep, and why I thanked the banished gods they gave me an excuse, a way out that I might use it as a shield against the love that still tries to cling to life inside my shattered chest.

Is that survival? Is that instinct? There is that part of me, an older and selfish part, that understands the words the demoness used and wants to live no matter the cost. Is it my inner strength or just a sickness in my mind brought on by trauma?

Whatever the case, I drank, and now I can only look forward as the past is denied to me forever.

She stood with the others, naked, chained, and brought forward in a long line. Nowin was before her. Her companion had been strangely silent the past day, the toll of the trails pressing down her shoulders and bowing her head as they marched on across the sands.

The bulk of the camp lay behind them. Now only stone structures remained, ancient ruins that marked the true boundary to what was once the old Leopard Hills capital. Ruks led them, the stink of earth drifting among the sands and the acidic tang of green fire clung to flesh and air in a kind of stinging haze.

The green tower of flame stretching to heaven from the city now dominated everything, the light forcing their eyes downward as the hiss of its energy played out like a million serpents slithering over the dunes.

A repetitive drone of a hammer punctuated each step the slaves took, men and women alike drawn ever forward until Caroline could see the genesis of the noise.

Buildings, most shielded with heavy tarps, stood around a huge anvil. Beyond the anvil rose a gate that made the Grand Entry of the ancient city of Tristra look small in comparison.

Banished Gods, how could a city like this have ever fallen?

Beyond the gate the green glow shimmered and swam, some unseen force holding it just inside the verge as the black basalt walls and towers of the defensive work that stared down, looming in mirthless oppression.

At the anvil a huge beast towered, half-man half-boar, with arms like corded steel and a hammer the size of an adult Ruk clutched in one black fist. It beat away at a chain that stretched from the anvil into the emerald maw of the gate, inexorably drawn forward as Ruks moved more links from the fire to the smith.

Caroline was pushed forward, those in front of her taken to the anvil where their bonds were attached to the chain, the length pulling them on, some of them struggling while others shambled without any emotion. Struggling or defeated, all went nonetheless.

The ringing of the hammer pounded her ears, all else drowned out as she was attached to the chain, Nowin still before her as she went forward. The battlements rose up fifty feet, towers half-again that size, the green glow spilling down over them in a kind of mist that coated weathered lions and eagles chiseled into the stone at every arch or corner.

Her stomach – unsettled still from her night of tangled dreams – churned, and she wavered on her tired legs but the chain would not be denied.

Ahead, a man raved and screamed as he was drawn through and silenced.

Please, let this be the end, for I fear I can take no more.

The acid of the glow touched her skin, burned her eyes, and choked her lungs, but ahead Nowin finally turned. Her stalwart defender's body was wreathed in the terrible light, but she called out just as she was drawn fully into the curse, "Do whatever it takes to survive!"

Then Nowin was gone, and the haze slithered around the bindings and the chain as words drifted from her lips as well.

"I promise!" she said, unsure if anyone was there to hear.

Light, then darkness, followed by a feeling of slimy water pressing across every inch of her body brought bile to her throat. Caroline gagged, stumbled forward, and still the chain continued to drag her along.

Coughing, she blinked away the dark, as a nightscape of tinted shadows spilled out around her. The sky twinkled with strange stars and colorful planets that dangled so close they looked like moons.

Impossible.

The chain moved on, and although five links down the line were visible in the near-dark, no Nowin or any other captive stood attached.

"Hello?" she whispered.

Somewhere in the darkness a low rumbled brewed, and she pulled against her bonds, the scrape of the metal echoing in the abandoned entry.

A smell wafted to her, the scent a mix of sweat and sulfur, a shape pulling away from a wall and drawing out into the starlight. It was large, ten foot at the apex of its horned head and thickly muscled. One red eye, smote with a black iris, looked about the chain until it settled on her. She pulled harder, her mouth dry and gooseflesh prickling up her arms.

It took a step, the bowed legs knobbed at the knee and a tangle of red hair at its groin was cut with genitals that rivaled a Mountainback in heat.

"Help!" she screamed.

The beast drew closer, and the stink of it gagged her, the breath blown from its lungs like an enveloping blanket of rotting flesh.

One hand, clawed with yellow nails, reached out and took the link connecting her bonds to the greater chain and shattered it like glass.

Her knees buckled, and the creature lifted her up, a wide nose the size of her waist sniffing her up and down until it threw her over a shoulder and marched off into the night.

She struggled, raised her head, blinked as the backward facing journey made her eyes swim. Buildings passed by, all of dark stone, some fallen in and others closed and built up like small stockades. Around the structures things lurked, lizard-like and winged with the same red eyes as the beast that carried her.

What abyss have I fallen to?

No pedestrian walked the crumbled streets where grey sand piled up in alleys. Before Caroline's meager breakfast was forced out her throat, the thing lifted her once more.

She dangled in the open air a moment and was then laid upon the cobbles, a single violet lamp burning brightly above her head. Shivers tore through her, the stink having permeated her flesh and the nausea making her swallow again and again as the creature waited.

Looking up, she saw his maleness presented so close she could have reached out and touched it. Gagging, she turned away, and from somewhere behind a bolt was thrown and a door creaked open.

"Is it her?" a voice asked.

"She smells of nobility," the beast rumbled.

"Excellent, I can take it from here."

Bowed legs lumbered away, and Caroline took a deep breath, the acrid air of the city a blessing compared to the odor of the gatekeeper.

"Caroline?" the voice asked.

Turning, she saw a woman standing in the light of a circular doorway. She was tall, with honeyed hair that spilled down past her thin waist and skin that twinkled all along its golden surface.

"How do you know me?" Caroline asked.

The woman smiled, teeth white and perfect, saying, "It's me, Torna."

Caroline shook her head, "I don't know that name."

Leaving the door, the woman looked up and down the dark street, her movements as fluid as a dancers steps, the meager fabric of her silken clothing hiding only the most private parts of her body.

She walked forward and offered Caroline a hand. "It's not safe on the street, come with me and we can talk, at least for a few minutes before your summons."

Caroline looked at the woman's hand, the golden skin trailing down to long fingernails studded with diamonds and painted a delicate shade of white.

"Come, we've little time, I know, but it's important you come with me before the doorman arrives," Torna said.

Nodding, Caroline took her hand. A spark exchanged in the touch and her eyes widened. A vision sprang up in her mind, the dirty and common visage of a young woman in a cage, ragged and alone.

"Torna!" Caroline whispered.

Torna squeezed her hand, "You do remember, good, at least my wait hasn't been for naught."

Caroline looked up, Torna's eyes shaded with white paint that bled back toward her studded ears. Beyond the paint the rich brown irises stood out, shone in the violet light of the lamp, and the soul of the slave who had delivered her a message of Nowin two days before still lurked there.

"How?" Caroline asked.

"I'll tell you, but not now. First, you must come with me. Mistress Alanthria will have to take a look at you and I want you to impress her, because if you don't... well, let's not think like that."

"I don't understand," Caroline said.

Torna pulled her from beneath the light, the round door swallowing them both before the woman drew it closed and barred it with a heavy bolt. After the bar was in place, she whispered a word and runes blazed to life on the surface, each one touched with a skull at the center.

"It took three decades to get the password to that door, but you're here, so it was worth it," Torna said.

Caroline furrowed her brow but the woman pulled her on, the corridor dimly lit as it twisted several times before coming to another round portal. Torna opened this one, peeked inside, and then drew Caroline on, the passage beyond one of polished white marble that ran with veins of gold and violet.

Their bare feet made no sound as they slipped along the corridor, Torna passing several more round doors before opening one painted green and set with silver scrollwork around the knob. They entered, the chamber filled with steam and the smell of honey. A cascade of water flowed at one side into a shallow pool, and Torna pulled her to it before waiving her forward.

"Go," she said handing her a bar of scented soap.

Caroline gingerly touched the water's surface, but it was warm and inviting, the feel of it slippery and a thin sheen of oil created a circular rainbow around her ankle when she placed her foot on the first sunken step. She moved under the spillway, the water washing over her like a dream and she let it touch every inch as she turned back and forth inside the fall.

"I remember my first bath," Torna said. "It was like a dream, like everything that had happened in my life was washed clean of my soul."

Caroline brought the soap up and drank in its flavor, the scent unfamiliar but sweet. It bubbled between her fingers, the harsh lye scrubs she was used to forgotten as she slid it over her body.

"I know, I talk too much, always have. My mother used to whip me with a switch when I'd pester her as she worked in the garden or tended to my brothers and sisters," Torna said.

Sighing, Caroline opened her eyes and looked once more on the woman before her. Torna was tall, more so than the last time she'd seen her, and each curve of her body was flawless, as was her strange skin. Her hair, once as short and tattered mess, was now luxuriant as that of the highest Ushan princess, finely oiled with long impossible curls. Breasts once petite had become round and full, and the width of her waist had cinched as her hips had smoothed out in rounded perfection.

"You can't be her," Caroline said.

Torna smiled, Caroline's skin prickling and her nipples tightening at the display. She covered herself, dipped further into the falling water.

"I know I've changed. I mean, Torna is dead, she died the day I came into the city. Now I'm Ixis, Carnal of the 2nd House and Key Keeper of the delivery door."

"How can that be?" Caroline asked.

"It's hard to understand, but time moves differently in the Burning City," Torna/Ixis replied.

The water continued to fall, and Caroline started shaking even in the warmth of the flow.

"How differently?" she asked.

Ixis moved to a table filled with heavy towels and pulled one from the pile. She came back and offered it to Caroline. Cautiously, she came out of the water and pulled the fabric around her. It was soft as a cloud and drew the water away from her skin without becoming wet itself.

"How differently?" she asked again.

"Until today I didn't know the truth, but your appearance has confirmed the rumors, at least to me."

There was a pause, Caroline staring at Ixis until she sighed and continued, "This isn't good… I shouldn't say anything until after you meet Mistress Alanthria, but that's me talking too much yet again."

"Please Torna," Caroline said.

"Ixis…"

"Ixis." Caroline echoed.

"For every day that takes place outside the city, thirty-seven years passes within these walls."

Caroline shook her head, her legs losing their strength and Ixis caught her before she could fall.

"No…" she whispered.

"I'm sorry, I know it's a great deal to take in, but you kept asking and I, well, I…"

"Talk too much." Caroline finished, with her first genuine smile since her ordeal began.

Ixis laughed, but Caroline still clung to her, the nausea she'd had on the street returning as tears stung the corners of her freshly washed eyes.

Caroline was naked, but her bonds had been removed and her body was clean and scented with oil. The tears had dried and been brushed away as Ixis applied pigment around her eyes and then dressed her nails with violet paint.

A single gold chain was wrapped around her waist and hung loosely against her hips, the thin links sliding along her skin with each step.

Ixis walked beside her as they moved from a dressing area, several small creatures with mottled green skin coming and going around their legs as they walked.

"They are Lungins, indentured servants to the Apothecary. They tend to the cleaning and such, but you get used to them, so much so I don't even realize they're there anymore," Ixis said.

Caroline nodded, a lump still lingering in her throat.

Thirty-seven years? Oh Colin, even if you come for me now a lifetime will have passed before you reach these streets!

The hall was sparsely decorated, but spotless, the marble shining around them as they passed. Two women, both dressed in garb as unseemly as Ixis', watched them from a secluded divan, but Ixis paid them no mind as she continued on.

Two dozen round doors, all varying in color and trimmed in silver drifted past them, but the two of them finally stopped before a round double door. One panel was painted violet, and the other gold.

Ixis stepped forward, pulled a cord next to the door, and turned back to Caroline, whispering, "This is as far as I go, but remember, she likes to see the real you. I know this has been hard, but try to show the light inside you. I know it's still in there."

She backed away as a catch was thrown on the far side of the door and the panels swung inward, each on a single hinge. Beyond the portal was a room of dreams, the luxury of it glimmering like a dragon's hoard.

Vases painted with swirling designs of violet, pink, and white sat between pillars of glowing jade and twining golden serpents. The floors were polished and lacquered red planks set with silken rugs with patterns and colors to complement those of the walls.

Pillows, divans, and a bed the size of a king's table lay about the chamber, the headboard of the silk-laden sleeper decorated with a thousand peacock feathers. Gold, silver, and gems twinkled from crimson busts, as did gowns spun of darkness, moonlight, and strands of the sun.

Caroline took three tentative steps into the chamber before the door closed with a sucking hiss behind her. She turned, the portal's single polished bar sliding into place and the scent of perfume rising from incense burning in braziers on either side.

"Ixis speaks very highly of you," a sublime voice said.

Looking back into the chamber, Caroline saw a woman with violet skin and raven-wing hair seated at a richly appointed table. She must have been working as scrolls lay atop it as well as a serving of porcelain cups.

Caroline bowed as the woman, presumably Alanthria, leaned back in her cushioned chair.

"Come forward, I'd like to see you," Alanthria said.

Caroline did as she was instructed. The rugs were soft and warm beneath her feet, but the chamber held a chill that tightened her in places she fought not to cover.

"How old are you?" Alanthria asked.

"Nineteen winters."

"Married?"

"Yes."

"Have you known love?"

"Yes."

Alanthria sighed, took out a quill from a silver pot on her desk and wrote something on a scroll.

"I have no need of young, stupid, married girls. This note will deliver you elsewhere," she said.

Caroline shook her head, "No, I…"

"The doorman will see you to the street, from there, you can do as you please," Alanthria continued.

"Please!" Caroline screamed.

I remember the gatekeeper, the abandoned streets, and all the red eyes… what fate other than ruin would I face there? Better to be here, with a friend, than the unknown of the Burning City.

Alanthria's quill stopped writing, but she didn't look up. It hovered there for so long that Caroline lost track of time before the mistress spoke again.

"How old are you?" she asked.

Caroline bit her bottom lip, the silence deafening.

"How old are you?" Alanthria asked again.

"I don't know" Caroline answered.

"Are you married?"

"No."

"Have you ever been in love?"

"I have no idea what love is."

Alanthria drew the quill back from the parchment, as smile on her lips. She was beautiful, so much so the smile made Caroline's heart race in her chest.

"What is your name?" Alanthria asked.

"Caro…" she paused, continued. "I have no name."

Nodding, Alanthria stood and walked around the desk. She was clothed in a fabric that moved like a second skin, the material clinging to the curves of her body without care of gravity or any other principle of science.

When she drew close, Caroline had to look up at her. The woman was as impossibly tall as Colin, seven feet and powerful. Her muscles were lean and well-defined beneath her supple, violet skin.

Taking Caroline's hands in hers, Alanthria exchanged no spark, but her eyes flared with an amber glow.

"You are lovely, more so than most who are brought before me," Alanthria said.

Caroline lowered her eyes, "I'm nothing compared to the women I've seen."

"No, dearest, you're more than them because you've come to me already lovely, and the transformations you see are profound but can only add to what is already in place," Alanthria said.

The mistress touched her chin, lifted her face so that she could draw close, her breath smelling like berries in the spring, "I will make you a goddess, but only you can make yourself special. Do you understand?"

Caroline nodded.

"And I shall name you Shay. In this place which has given you birth and is both mother and father to you, I get the privilege of this birthright, so use the name I've given you wisely my newborn daughter."

A single tear slipped down Caroline's cheek, and Alanthria caught it with a finger, brought it before her dark eyes and asked, "What is your name?"

"Shay," Caroline whispered.

"Good, Shay, you may go, and tell Ixis I want you prepared for the Sanctuary in a month," Alanthria said.

Behind her the bolt on the door was thrown open by unseen hands and the double doors swung inward.

Bowing, Shay backed up until she was on the far side. Once there, the door quickly shut, the bar sliding back into place. She gave a great sigh, her chest aching and she wiped further tears from the corners of her eyes.

"I see you've passed," Ixis said.

Her friend appeared from an alcove to the side of the door, a smile on her golden lips.

"My name is Shay" she whispered.

"A lovely name, and is there anything else?" Ixis asked.

"Yes, you are to have me ready for the Sanctuary in a month," Shay said.

Ixis raised an eyebrow.

"What is it?" Shay asked.

"A month is very fast, faster than I've ever seen a new girl go into the Sanctuary, so you must have impressed the mistress."

Shay didn't reply, and Ixis took her hand and led her back down the hall, the woman spouting off meaningless tidbits of information concerning every colored door they passed.

CHAPTER EIGHT

COLIN

Sleep doesn't come easy, and when it does I'm plagued with dark dreams I cannot put voice to.

She suffers, I know it, and for some reason I believe you know it as well. The failing is mine, as is the burden of guilt, and yet I take each step forward hoping against hope that I can somehow make this right.

I'm a believer in fate, if not in the banished gods, and I want there to be a reason for things, but for the life of me I see no silver lining in this. My home is gone, my province ravaged, and my people dead or scattered to the wind. My wife, the dearest treasure in my life, is taken by slavers and carried ever north to a doom I can't even begin to imagine.

What would you do, Observer? No answer, of course, and I expected none, but still I feel a glimmer of some decision in you which tells me you're more human than you realize.

Colin leaned against a tree, his eyes closed and a hand pressed against the bandage at his thigh. Behind him the screams had stopped and Dula's incessant pacing along with it. Thorn sat beside him, and Luur was off among the tattered tents, an occasional howl and clang of combat coming from camp.

"There are more than three dozen slaves, and I've no idea what to do about them," Thorn said.

Colin opened his eyes, the sun falling away in a blaze of red to the west and the Ghost Moon already showing its face on the horizon to the east. He paused, put two fingers in his mouth and then gave a sharp whistle.

A howl was returned from the camp and he sighed, saying, "I'll get Luur back here before he hunts down every non-slave in the camp. If we leave a few they should watch over the slaves."

"Watch over them? You mean we're going to leave them here?" Thorn asked.

"We are on a mission, and they can't be our concern. If we free them, supply them, and turn them loose, how long will they last in these sands?" Colin answered.

Thorn turned back to the cages outlined on the far edge of the dune valley, his head shaking.

"I don't like this. Light cannot possibly defeat the darkness if it is lessened by taking shadow inside itself," Thorn said.

"I respect that, and yet the reality of the situation means I either save them or save Caroline, and as much as it might seem selfish and cruel, I'm going to choose my wife every time," Colin said.

"I could…" Thorn began but was cut short when Roma walked out of the trees.

The Wizard was damp, the fabric at his shoulders darker than the hem of his robes, and his sleeves were rolled up and dripping at the elbow.

"I've got what we need," Roma said.

Colin turned, winced, and then lay back, saying, "Then speak as the day draws to a close."

Roma came forward and offered Colin a vial of clear liquid, "Here, this will help with the pain, but only take a sip, the potion is valuable."

Drawing out the stopper, Colin smelled the liquid but it held no scent. He lifted it, took a small swig and felt a shock run through his system as light shown from inside the bandage on his thigh.

"God magic," he whispered.

Roma shook his head, "No, the gods are gone, as is their blessing, but there are other ways to restore a body with magic."

"He means necromancy," Dula said.

Colin looked up at the Wizard, his leg shifting in the process but there was no pain.

"What is this?" he asked.

"A soul," Roma began, "Or at least the distilled essence of one."

Colin held it away from himself as he replaced the stopper. Beside him Thorn asked, "Where did you get it."

"The prisoner volunteered it, but before you give me the look already creeping across your face, know that he deserved everything he got, and his final act will be to provide us healing when it is sorely needed," Roma said.

Colin handed the vial back to the Wizard.

"This is madness," Thorn said.

Luur came bounding up to the party, blood still dripping from his axe and the better part of his body covered in a browning layer of the stuff.

"You called?" he asked.

Colin got to his feet, tested the leg and then nodded. "Yes, I think we may have news and I didn't want you killing everyone, no matter how much they deserve it."

"Roma, what have you found?" Colin asked.

"The Ruk was a lead trader, his contact in a place called The Embers is a demon named Ilcanth, and she's the one to whom Caroline was delivered," Roma answered.

"How was she?" Colin asked.

Roma shook his head, "I could tell you, but I'd rather simply suggest that the fate which befell the Ruk at my hands was well deserved."

Colin's stomach churned, bile coming to this throat.

"What of Nowin?" Thorn asked.

"Much the same. Both were taken to The Embers two days ago, perhaps less if you don't count the night quickly approaching."

"Luur, can we risk the sands at night?" Colin asked.

The Lowl shook his head, "I wouldn't, the day is dangerous enough, but if you must my nose could follow a trail if provided."

Colin cursed and looked north.

I'm coming for you, I promise.

"How long to The Embers?" Colin asked.

"Two days on foot, half that if we have ride," Roma said.

Colin turned to the south of the camp, a collection of mighty Mountainbacks lurking in a stable there.

"What about them?" he asked.

"What about them?" Thorn repeated.

"Could they make the trip at night?" Colin asked.

Dula stepped forward, saying, "You might be right. If they make the journey from here to The Embers regularly, it might be burned into their minds, and it would cut our travel time."

"Can you ask them?" Colin asked.

She nodded, and Colin signaled Thorn to go with her as she moved off to the pens. He turned to Luur, saying, "If we're going on Mountainback, they'll be skittish enough with you around, so go clean yourself in the pool."

Luurs nodded and slunk into the trees and Colin looked at Roma as the Wizard slowly unrolled his sleeves, the water in them having dissipated.

"I want you to tell me what the Ruk confessed," he said.

"It will not help you," Roma replied.

"I know, but I will know it nonetheless."

Roma nodded, the story of the corrupting earth slowly rolling from him lips.

The Mountainback lurched back and forth with every step, Colin sitting on an empty cage that the beast dragged like a carriage across the sands. Above, the Ghost Moon waned and the Blood was rising above its larger sister. On the northern horizon a green glow had appeared that coalesced into a sliver of emerald leading up into the sky.

He took a swig of water from his skin, the retching he'd done before they departed the settlement leaving him spent.

"What is that?" Thorn asked.

"The Burning City," Roma answered.

"That's impossible. We're far too many miles away to see its light," the bowman muttered.

"Nothing is impossible, trust me, and it is indeed the glow of the city."

"But how?" Thorn asked.

"Legend tells that once the curse was enacted, a green fire burst from the outer walls of the city and burned upward directly into the heavens. If we are closing in on The Embers, then that glow must still be the tower of flame that has burned for ninety-one years," Roma answered.

"Then this is the Leopard Hills," Colin said.

No one replied, all eyes going out to the endless dunes.

Finally Luur started snoring, and Colin fell into his own twisted dreams. He fought against dark powers, his sword too slow, but then Thorn shook him awake, the sun breaching in the East and the grey sands touched with gold along their ridges.

"The Embers," Thorn pointed.

Colin rubbed sleep and sand from the corners of his eyes, the dunes ahead giving way to a series of dark ruins. Smoke rose from several tents and buildings, and the thin emerald tower from the night before had been replaced with a swath of green flame that dominated the northern horizon and folded back ominously over their heads.

"Banished Gods!" he exclaimed.

"I feel you my friend," Thorn said. "I believe this is as close to Hell as we're ever likely to get."

"I wouldn't take such a bet if I were you," Roma said.

Luur drew up close, axe in his hand. "What are we doing once we get inside? This place looks a lot more heavily guarded than the last outpost."

Colin watched the growing camp, more a small city than anything else. Finally, he looked under the tarp beneath them, a dozen slaves holding each other close in the cage. Resigned, he took a great breath.

"We'll do as planned, offer the slaves up as the next shipment for Ilcanth and see if it works, or if we can at least gain an audience with her. If not, let's hope there's an open water source and no other Wizards about."

"Do you want me to have a look around the camp, maybe try to smell Nowin or Caroline out?" Luur asked.

Colin nodded, "If they let us in, yes, see what you can find. Whatever happens in there, if we get separated, fall back to this entry point at sundown, understood?"

The company nodded, the Mountainback pulling them on through the town as robed and armed citizens moved out of the way. No eye paid them any mind, and the Mountainback walked a slow path toward an even larger collection of cages stacked in a maze at one side of the town.

From the top of the cage Colin could make out black walls in the distance, the green fire blazing up from them and the constant sound of a hammer and anvil split the morning air.

"Ho!" a man's voice called.

The Mountainback came to a halt and Colin stood and moved forward on the stretched tarp that covered the cage. He met the gaze of a tanned man with pale eyes and thin black hair that receded up his scalp almost to the crest.

"What service is this?" the man asked.

"A shipment for Ilcanth," Colin said.

The man looked at the slaves within, saying, "Ilcanth wasn't expecting a shipment so soon. Who brought the order?"

"We are independent contractors new to the trade and the Ruk..." he paused.

Roma whispered, "Olovo."

"Olovo," Colin continued. "Set us on the trail."

The man frowned, but waved them down.

"I'll have to record you in the ledger, and I've seen better slaves, especially for Ilcanth, but if Olovo wants to deliver unsuitable wares, then that's his problem," the man said.

Colin descended the bars, his boots puffing up sand as he hit the ground. Beyond the cage a group of armored men appeared, marching in quick step with long spears held in their hands.

"Roma," Colin said.

"I've got them," the Wizard replied.

The soldiers came up short, the leader stepping forward and giving a slight bow, saying, "Ilcanth provides you a greeting and wishes to see you and the Wizard in her tents. The rest of your company can find food, drink, and entertainment in the Emerald's Shadow if they wish."

Colin looked at Roma who shrugged his shoulders.

"As Ilcanth wishes," Colin said. "Roma, you're with me and the rest of you enjoy yourselves."

Luur gave a ready howl and Thorn nodded, Colin moving forward to accompany the men back into the heart of the camp. Roma fell in beside him, the man smelling of the deep ocean, a scent that made Colin's skin crawl.

Around them the soldiers cleared a path, the patrons of the town stepping away as the procession moved with purpose toward a huge tent that dominated the central pinwheel of the community.

When they reached the main opening, two heavily armed Ruks pulled the flaps open and Colin and Roma walked in alone. The room was filled with finery and a lone man waited within, his long coat buttoned with a high collar looking out of place in the desert setting.

The man smiled. Each one of his white teeth sharpened to a point, and the irises of his eyes were a bright violet that bled to green around the edges.

"The mistress wants to welcome you to The Embers, and congratulates you for your fortitude and determination to get here. It's not often anyone follows their lost people into these unforgiving wastes," the man said.

"They are more than our people," Colin spat.

The man tipped his head, "Indeed, which is why she's invited you both to treat with her and let the others languish with the unwashed masses."

The man motioned Roma to a series of pillows and a tray of colorful fruit and wine that sat in the middle of it.

"Won't you have a seat, Master Wizard, as the first guest to the mistress's private abode will be the Fleetwood."

The hairs on Colin's neck stood on end, but before he could protest Roma bowed and moved to the tray, his fingers picking among the fruit until he chose a plum.

"After you," the man said motioning Colin to the far side of the chamber.

He moved forward, the man one step in the lead as he drew back a flap that opened into a central wheel with the green-tinged sky bright above.

"The lady's solarium, but she'll be meeting you in her inner sanctum, which I must tell you is a special privilege," the man said.

There is nothing special about any of this.

The man moved on and led Colin to one of the inner flaps that surrounded the solarium. With a wave, he motioned him through.

It took a moment for his eyes to adjust, but the smell of the place was potent and his palms broke out in a sweat after the first breath.

Blinking, he squinted and made out the shape of a bed that was surrounded by a mix of skulls and violet orchids. A woman languished among the sheets, her flesh naked save for a black cape that slipped from her shoulders and bled out in inky darkness upon the violet sheets.

"Greetings, Fleetwood, I have waited more years than you would know for your family to return," she said.

The tremor of her voice slithered into his ear and made his heart pound, the spark in his chest lighting as heat spilled off him. He swallowed, fingers flexing, and his loins coming to life beneath the codpiece of his armor.

Get out of my head! This is a demon's glamour. Keep control you fool!

"I've come for my wife," he said.

His voice was thin, raspy, and there was no force behind the words.

She smiled and his heart broke in his chest. His left foot took a tentative step forward before he shook his head and backed away three footfalls to the tent's flap.

Her smile continued as she said, "It's true, about the will of your family, any lesser man would have already been groveling at my feet by now and certainly not backing toward my door."

"I've come for my *wife*," he repeated.

This time the words were louder, more weight carried with them and he took a deep breath and cooled his inner fire.

"She isn't here," Ilcanth replied.

"Then where is she?"

"The City of course. Had I known you were coming I would have kept her, but since this is the first time anyone has ever made it this far you must fully understand my unwillingness to deny my purse with the coin she was worth."

Colin reached over his shoulder for his blade and Ilcanth's smile grew.

"Will you punish me?" she asked impishly.

Drawing a hand over her breasts she lowered her eyes and again the heat inside him boiled up.

Keep your head! She's playing a game.

"I've come for my wife," he repeated, not trusting himself to say anything more complicated.

Her smile faded, but only a little, "I always thought Fleetwoods were supposed to be smart?"

Her patronizing anger kindled his spark. "You mistake my statement for stupidity, when I mean it as a truth. If you don't have her, then there is nothing I need from you so I will go."

"Oh but there is," she said.

He frowned, "Don't play with me, if I've gotten all the way here, I'm more dangerous than you know."

"Spoken like a true Fleetwood. The Empress would be so proud," she yawned.

His knees ached, and he forced his feet to stay set, but his desire leaked out of him from sweat that trickled down the side of his face.

"Speak!" he yelled.

"Very well. Your wife now resides inside the Burning City, it's true, but a sword and the will of a lion won't bring her back because the power of the curse is too strong, even for you."

He waited, and she slowly turned in the bed, the cloak at her shoulders moving with her until it flared slightly and the shape of two leathery wings spread around her.

"I have magic that will protect you, get you inside, but it will cost you a price that your wife has already paid, although she had less choice than you."

"What price?"

"I want your oath," she answered.

"My oath? Don't speak in riddles as I haven't the time."

"Very well, I want you to share my bed, and break your wedded vow to your wife so that you might still have a chance to save her."

"I would never…"

She cut him off, "Don't speak words you can't take back. I give you the one and only chance you will ever have to find her, if she truly means that much to you, then my infinitely simple price is nothing more than words spoken before an impotent and godless priest.

"It is a gift, I promise you, and one you'd not get from anyone else in this camp or perhaps on the face of this world, but I have strange tastes. Think hard, Fleetwood, because this offer won't last long. Do you truly love her, or some pledge made from the dreams of romantics and fools?"

Banished Gods, what demon's bargain is this? I should kill this creature, take her secrets, but without Roma there is no way to be sure of the truth or lies in it. If I fail, I could lose Caroline forever… and that I cannot take.

Ilcanth continued, "I will accept one night of service from you, from dusk till dawn, and when it is done I will deliver the means for you and three of your companions to survive the entry into the city to pursue your love to your heart's content, otherwise I promise that the city's curse will destroy you before you take your tenth step."

She's bartering, which means she's scared, but she also holds all the power in the end, and if I do this I spare my companions the weight of such dark bargains on their souls.

"Three companions?" he asked.

"Yes, the Wizard will have to buy his own ticket into the gate, but that will be between him and me."

Silence settled between them, the woman's wings pulsing black and silky in the dim light. Finally, she asked, "What is your answer?"

Caroline, what bargain did she take from you? What sacrifice must I make to win you back, and what greater tragedies will you endure to stay alive for me?

Slowly, he released his grip on his blade, "I'll do it."

Smiling, she rolled over, stepped off the bed and walked to a dressing screen.

"You may return at dusk, my man will let you inside," she said.

He stood, his head shaking back and forth.

"You may go," she called over the screen.

Go? Where do I go, other than to a hell of my own making?

CHAPTER NINE

CAROLINE

My name is Caroline, no matter what they tell me. I was not re-born here. I'm the same girl raised in the wilds of Western Gariny, married to a man of my choosing, and bound as a slave but never conquered.

This world, this city, is like a dream, a nightmare, and although I play within the confines of its rules I can't accept it because I feel it is all a house of lies.

I'll play the part, because I have no other choice, but no matter the mask I wear I will always remember my name and where I came from. I will hold to that, because without that tether I know the madness would sweep me away and drown me in a lucid oblivion.

So I am to be a plaything of men, a whore to the city, and my pledge to the man I love broken irrevocably. But I will endure, and I will keep my promise, because these dooms may take my body, but Colin, my husband, they will never take my love, no matter how much anguish they perpetrate upon me.

Yes, Nowin, I will survive…

Caroline sat in a cushioned chair, Lungins toiling over her nails and hair, the small creatures whispering incoherently to each other as they did their work. Beside her Ixis sat, regal and golden, the Lungins attending her as well.

"So what do you think of your first week inside the Apothecary?" Ixis asked.

"I spent five years in the Imperial Finishing Academy in Nextyaria. This isn't much different," she answered.

"Truly?"

"No, in reality the Academy was a hundred times as demanding."

Ixis turned to look at her, a Lungin raising its voice in protest but she waved it away.

"Well, I'll admit I'm being a bit easy on you, but there is much more to work with than most women we get here so the ease works both ways," Ixis said.

"How many others have you trained?" Caroline asked.

"Dozens, most thriving, but there are others that have been lost along the way," Ixis answered.

"Lost?"

Leaning back, Ixis waved the Lungin to return, saying, "The Sanctuary is like any other place in the city – which is to say lethal – and it must be navigated accordingly."

"When will I see the Sanctuary?" Caroline asked.

"Next week if all continues as planned, but first we must discuss your experience, a topic I thought better left until you were more comfortable," Ixis said.

"I can't imagine being less comfortable than I am now," Caroline said.

"Perhaps in body, and in the moment, but I've heard you at night. I would like to understand your dreams before I move you onto the subject of the Sanctuary. It's typically why the Sanctuary waits for more than a single month, most women requiring more time to heal before they enter the carnal house. Alanthria either had great faith in you or she wants to break you quickly and be done with you."

Caroline turned, one of her Lungin pulling her hair, and she hissed and looked back forward. After some time she said, "I didn't know you could hear me, at night I mean."

"It's my job to prepare you, both body and mind, and without the mind you won't make it far. Some girls can't get over what's happened to them, and in the Sanctuary that translates to a quick death.

"I know what happened out there still lurks like a fresh wound, but I can help you with it if you'll let me. Remember, I lived it the same as you," Ixis said.

Tears welled up in the corners of her eyes, the fresh paint the Lungins had painstakingly applied threatened with ruin as she tried to blink them back.

"I don't think you understand what happened," Caroline said.

Her voice shook and broke half way through the sentence, but she managed to get it all out without the tears falling.

"Perhaps not, but I surely won't until you tell me," Ixis said.

The Lungins continued their work, Caroline closing her eyes, breathing, and waiting until the tremors and emotions stopped fighting.

At last she said, "I was violated."

"Dear Shay, my sister, we were all violated."

"No, the Ruk, he forced himself inside me with his earth..." she trailed off the word catching in her throat.

"Earth?" Ixis asked.

Caroline nodded, the Lungin hissing at her.

"I take it that was your first time?"

"Yes."

"It's painful, torturous if truth be told, but you can get used to it, I promise you. There are others of our world here, and their elements sometimes weigh against ours. You must acquiesce, and hope they know well enough to keep your spark lit or..." Ixis trailed off.

Caroline was silent, thinking '*or I am lost*'

Banished Gods, I'll never get used to it, I can still feel it all around me, the night terrors waking me without remorse as I feel the pain again and again...

"One thing we must ingrain in ourselves is that sex and love are two distinctly separate entities. If you distance yourself from the Human conception that is has some greater meaning and simply see the act as the same as tilling a field, cooking a meal, or carrying a load to market, the burden of it will fall away," Ixis continued.

I think I'm going to be sick...

"May I ask how experienced with sex you were before the Ruk?" Ixis interrupted.

"What the Ruk did wasn't sex!" Caroline protested.

Her reply was much louder than she'd intended, the Lungins jumping back and two other women, one with silver skin and one pales as ice, looked from chairs close by. Ixis smiled and waved them back to their preparations.

"It is, in its way, and the sooner you realize that, the better it will be for you," Ixis said.

A tear fell from Caroline's left eyes, and the Lungin hissed and caught it with a thin white cloth before it made it to her chin.

"Tell me about your dreams?" Ixis asked.

Caroline shook her head, more tears falling. The Lungins drew back, a hissing conversation played out among them before Ixis clapped her hands and sent them away. Her golden fingers reached out and touched hers, the contact making her pull away but Ixis caught her and wouldn't let go.

"You have to move past it. I know it's asking a lot so soon. When I came here it took me six months to walk the Sanctuary and another three before I made it to the floor. I truly didn't think I could survive it, and I was a hundred times more experienced in the ways of these things than you, and you have only a fraction of the time I had.

"When I was eleven winters my uncle sat me on his lap and ran his hand up my skirt. At thirteen two boys from over the hill pressed me against a creek bank and took my virginity as I cried to the banished gods to stop them. By fifteen I'd started laying with the Baker's son to keep other boys at bay. If there is love and lifelong devotion, it's as much a fey tale as the dragon and the princess or the loom that spins thread into gold.

Caroline turned, the tears flowing freely now, "I... I'm sorry..."

Ixis rose, pulled Caroline from her seat and held her as the shakes rattled her bones.

"Tell me what happened, every detail, and hold nothing back. Only by getting it out can you pass to the other side, and remember, I'm your friend and I always will be," Ixis said.

Words slipped from Caroline's lips, halting, tear-choked, and bitter words, but they came nonetheless, and all the while Ixis held her. When it was done, Ixis walked her back to her chamber, closed the light-blue door, and extinguished the crystal lantern.

She lay with her in the dark, and for the first time in a week Caroline slept, no dreams plaguing her as the true exhaustion of her ordeal finally took her deep into the womb of sleep.

Ixis stood away, a fingernail raised to her black lips and one eye closed. Caroline watched her, several Lungin spitting unintelligible words at three human-sized spiders at one side of the room that deftly spun silk in a kind of dance.

"I don't know how a real woman has that waist," Ixis said.

"My mother said it was my grandmothers, and that she was favored by many men," Caroline answered.

"I can imagine."

The Lungins pressed Caroline's elbows with sticks and she raised her arms, her body naked as always.

Caroline looked at the spinners, the great spiders working at a fevered pace. They were large things, fully the size of a grown man and brown as newly tilled earth, with streaks of olive green wrapping their distended torsos. Where their silk threads touched the tips of their legs a blue spark shown, and some magic therein finished the silk to a perfect clothing quality material.

"How do they know what to spin?" she asked.

"They read your mind, or the mind of the Lungins, whichever matters to them at the moment," Ixis said.

"Truly?"

"Yes, it's not like we have tailors or designers in-house. The City can't provide the bodies for that, but we do have these arachnid master-weavers, and if you can imagine it, they can spin it," Ixis answered.

A Lungin prodded her, and she turned at an odd angle, the little thing's stick running across her backside.

"Since we have time while the fitters get your measurements, can we continue?" Ixis asked.

Caroline nodded.

"This isn't a trick question, and I'm not Alanthria, but I need to know if you've only been with one man?" Ixis asked.

"Yes."

"How many times?"

"Twice, both on our wedding night."

Ixis's mouth fell open and her eyebrows rose, "You're serious?"

"Yes."

"Then you haven't?"

Caroline turned, asking, "What?"

"Fetched metal?"

"What?" Caroline asked.

Ixis shook her head, whispering, "Banished Gods, a month is impossible…"

"What are you talking about?" Caroline asked.

"I'm talking about pleasure!" Ixis said.

The woman's normal peace was broken and a she stepped forward, a finger waving in the air.

"If you've only been with a man under heat of passion twice, then you can't have fetched metal, and without that it's impossible to train you!"

"I have no idea what you're talking about."

Ixis drew close, "That's the problem." The woman stepped back and looked down at the lead Lungin, demanding, "How long?"

The creatures jumped about, cast strange words at her, and the spiders stopped spinning. Ixis raised her hands, took two more steps back and the entire room returned to work.

"When this is done, I'm going to show you something that I hope will change everything you've ever understood about life," Ixis said.

Caroline watched her, the Lungins measuring and the spiders spinning, as a butterfly tickled the inside of her stomach.

The room was dark, the sound of water trickling down a stone-studded wall the only noise as the violet lantern pulsed gently against one wall. Caroline sat on a cushioned mat on the floor, and Ixis slid in behind her, the woman's naked body making her momentarily pull away.

"It's ok, I promise," Ixis said.

Caroline took in a long breath and then leaned back, the touch of Ixis taught nipples against her back making her own stand up until she drew her hands over them. Their sparks tangled, the heat of their elemental nature playing against one another at the connection of the flesh.

"I want you to relax," Ixis said.

Taking another breath, Caroline closed her eyes. Ixis moved her hands away from her and then back, the smell of scented oil drifting to her nose. Her friend's fingers touched hers, coiled into them and then slid up her arms to the elbow. Behind her, Ixis's chin pushed aside her hair as her lips kissed along the smooth line behind her ear.

Caroline drew in a sharp breath, arched her back and tried to pull away but Ixis fingers moved from elbow to her stomach and neck and pulled her back. She opened her eyes, whispering, "No..."

Ixis lips were at her ear, "You have to trust me, it's the only way."

I've never lied to myself about what would be expected of me in return for the safety offered by this place, but now it's all become very real.

Tears once again welled in her eyes but she closed them, bit back her emotions and tried to relax.

Ixis kissed her again, her oiled hands slowly running down her neck and up her stomach, fingers circling the curve of her breasts.

Caroline kept breathing as Ixis's finger continued circling. The fire within her kindled and became hot as her frustration grew. The oil was slick, and the touching so smooth it was like ecstasy, but as Ixis touched her, she painstakingly avoided the nipples, her kisses gentle and long against her neck.

A sound crawled up out of Caroline's throat, something old and primal. It slithered out as a kind of moan, and she pressed back into Ixis, her own breasts pressed out.

Ixis complied with the movement, the tips of her fingers brushing Caroline's nipples slightly and then pulling away to twine around her breasts once more.

She cried out at the touch, a flare of pleasure driving down like a shock from her nipples to her loins and her legs twined against one another at the knee.

Tears vanished, the world hot and lost in a fog as Ixis touched her nipples again, this time longer before she again drew away.

Caroline groaned, bit her lower lip and clawed at the cushions beneath her.

Banished Gods, this can't be real.

One of Ixis's hands slid down her stomach, two fingers pressing between her thighs and she opened them up. A gasp fell from her lips as the fingers moved lower, slid along the edges of her sex and found the surface open and slick.

Ixis pressed her, brushed a nipple again as she worked along the soft folds with the other hand. Spasms rippled across the surface of Caroline's mind, her body lost as flares of white hot pleasure washed over her.

Ixis' insistent fingers quickly found the heart of her pleasure, and each minute brought more pressure and longer, deeper touches as she squirmed in the other woman's embrace.

Finally Ixis withdrew her wet hand and replaced it with a smooth warm stone. Caroline opened her eyes as Ixis placed the thing against her and it trembled to life. Panic swept through her again, but Ixis held her tight, one hand pinching a nipple as the trembling stone rubbed against her until spots appeared in her vision.

Another primal moan ripped from her chest, and a convulsion tore through her as the smooth stone settled against her, pressed, shook, and turned while Ixis rhythmically pinched and forced down her nipples.

Light flashed, and she screamed, her body lost in something beyond her control. Her cry was lost in the room, among the water, and inside time, as Ixis drew the stone away and then held her tight.

She was breathing hard, sweat beaded her forehead and she couldn't open her eyes.

"*That* is fetching metal," Ixis whispered.

Between breaths, Caroline could only manage as weak, "I…"

"This was not about love or marriage, so never confuse sex with those things, that's only what the priests want you to believe. Sex is what it is, an act, and it can be both beautiful and ugly, but once you understand that you can begin to control it.

"Sex is power, be it physical, emotional, or even elemental as the Ruk showed you. This power and release is what the Apothecary offers in the Sanctuary. Because of it, the Burning City isn't consumed by the dark rage that builds in the men who stalk the streets and defend the citadels. That release is the catalyst for peace, or at least balance, be it in a marriage or in random coupling that helps turn a murderous man into a benign one."

Caroline nodded, her mouth dry and her body aching for more.

"I used a tremor stone on you tonight because I had to be sure you understood what we do here. As a woman, unless you've actually fetched metal you can't possibly understand, and sometimes one believes they've made the fetch when they've only known the border of pleasure. It's hardest the first time, but now that you know what it truly is, you can find it again. Use the stone as you wish, and use it often. The more you know yourself, the better you might serve others. Do you understand?" Ixis asked.

Caroline nodded again, and Ixis kissed her on the back of the head and rose, her golden body slick with sweat.

"Now that you've fueled my flames, I'm off to the Sanctuary, and I'll see you on the morrow, but remember my words," Ixis said.

Her teacher closed the door, the water still spilling down the wall and the lamp pulsing as Caroline lay back on the cushion and stared at the ceiling.

Colin, the madness is coming and I don't know how to stop it.

CHAPTER TEN

COLIN

I remember when I was a boy. I was raised by a nurse, my mother and father both dead, and a coastal kingdom mine to rule in name only. It was lonely, cruel, and I wished many times I'd been born someone else.

Still, I was a Fleetwood, my bloodline the most famous and powerful all the world, so I was taken on my fourteenth name day to the Imperial capital of Nextyaria. There, I was punished by the other noble sons and daughters in every way their creative minds could come up with. If I thought my youthful home had been bad, the emotional torture of the capital was a hundred times worse.

It was there I met Thorn, a kindred soul. Together we survived, found who we were as men, and I was proud of that. Words and deeds didn't break me. I was too stronger, and yet now I face the greatest betrayal a husband can perpetrate against a wife, and I can't discover a way around it.

I must become everything I've always hated, commit the sins of my father, Erik, and lay with a woman – if you can truly call her that – who is not my wife. Is the cure worse than the sickness? If it was only me, I would end it, but I can't, not with Caroline still out there. This then is my doom, and when I find my wife again I must confess it...

Thorn stood at his side, the bowman shaking his head. Dula and Luur were back a few steps, both keeping quiet, and Roma sagged against his staff, the bones in his hands showing beneath his sallow skin.

"Don't do it, Colin. She'll do to you just like she did to Roma," Thorn said.

"No," Roma hissed, "She took from me a measure of my magic, but what she takes from him is far more dangerous."

Colin could see from the haunted look in the man's face that he was still pained by the price the succubus had demanded of him.

"See, the Wizard warns you and yet you still look to go!" Thorn continued.

"I have to go," Colin said.

"No you don't! We have no idea if either of them are still alive in that place and she's a succubus! How can you possibly trust a word that comes out of her mouth?" Thorn demanded.

"I don't have a choice. I made a vow to my wife and I'll see it through." Colin answered.

Thorn threw his hands in the air, "You made several vows, and you're about to break one to keep the other – but that doesn't seem to stop you."

Colin walked away, Thorn calling after him, "You can never get back what you lose in there!"

The words trailed after him, but he walked on, the last light of day spilling away over the dunes.

Ahead, the tent rose like a lurking crab, its black edges trimmed in a green glow and bits of flame tumbling around it from above. At the entrance two men waited, pikes in their hands and scarves covering their faces.

They saluted, pulled their weapons aside and he entered. Inside the confines of the entry soft scents played in a misty haze and a brass tub had been placed in the middle of the rug. He paused, a woman coming from the shadows with head bowed.

She was naked and lithe, two small horns peeking from her black hair at the forehead and her skin a mix of crimson along her curves. Her flesh grew pale everywhere else.

"Lord Fleetwood, I'm to bathe you in preparation for the night," she said.

"This wasn't a part of the bargain," he said.

She kept her head down, "I know not the words of this bargain, but this will please my mistress, and I would keep her thus for my sake."

Please her? I could give a fig about such things.

He walked forward, started around the tub, but the woman moved around with him, two small black wings flaring at her shoulders.

"Please, grant a slave this boon. Only suffering will be had otherwise, and I promise I will do you justice," she said.

He reached out, pushed her chin up until her eyes met his. They were violet and murky, the edges touched in a subtle green aura.

"What's your name?" he asked.

"There is power in a name, something I don't have," she said.

"Well, miss, I wouldn't see you suffer, and if your mistress requires this, at least it keeps me from her for some time so I will do as you wish."

A smile touched her lips, and the spark inside his breast heated.

She carries the same enchantments as her mistress! Be wary you fool.

"Thank you, Lord," she said.

He stood as she disrobed him, her nimble fingers making quick work of the laces binding his tunic and breeches. The smell of days of hard travel and combat spilled off him when he stood naked.

She touched his hand, drew him to the bath, and he stepped into the warm water. A sigh escaped his lips, the smell of it pure and sweet. He lay back and closed his eyes, the slave slipping her hands into the water as she drew a cloth across his skin.

Her work was long and slow, each inch of him cleaned until she made her way behind him and poured a pitcher of water over his hair. A frown touched his lips.

"Did you know in some cultures it's a sin to have a woman other than your wife wash your hair?" he asked.

"I was not aware, Lord," she said.

A honeyed and thick liquid was poured into his red tangles, and her fingers worked it in, his scalp tingling.

"Have you a wife?" she asked.

"Yes."

"Does she do this for you?"

He shook he head, "No, we've only been married a day."

"Then I will do my best that you may feel my fingers and think of her," she said.

A sigh escaped his lips, and he relaxed, the girl's fingers working some kind of magic into him they tended his tired muscles and eased his fractured mind.

Thrice she poured water into his locks, and twice more she mixed liquids until he was next to the door of slumber, but her hand touched his face and he opened his eyes.

"I will shave you," she said.

He nodded, her eyes drawing him in and her words slithering compliance into his ears. Dabbing a cream over his neck and jaw, she then brought forth a razor and slowly drew it across his skin.

The scrape of it was quick and she worked without pause, each stroke slicing a perfect strip out of the cream. When she was done, she snapped the razor shut with a click and stood.

"Rise, Lord, and I will rinse you," she said.

He nodded, and got to his feet. She brought forth more water, brushed him with it, until no space was left unattended.

"A fine job," he said.

She smiled again, his heart racing and blood rushing into places that turned her eyes from him as she walked to a stand and took up a heavy robe.

He stepped from the bath, took the garb and tied it around him. She bowed, and backed away with a hand waving to the central flap.

"The Lady awaits," she said.

He nodded and with a sigh marched through the far flap and into the solarium. A chunk of flame impacted over his head when he came under the open sky, the green fire oozing over an unseen barrier and sliding out of his line of sight.

He took a breath, adjusted his robe, and opened the flap to the chamber where he'd first met the sinful creature Ilcanth.

The chamber was lit with an amber glow, heat coiling out of braziers set in five positions around the great bed and a menagerie of succulents lay atop a table to the right of the room.

Ilcanth was nowhere to be seen, the dressing screen folded to one side of the bed and the violet sheets smoothed out like a sea of glass.

He moved forward, his palm wet and his heart pounding.

I don't know if I can do this.

Incense played in his nose, tendrils of smoke rising from sticks on a small stand to the left of the bed and a tall glass of clear red liquid beside it. He leaned down and looked through the fluid, a black insect suspended inside like a fly in amber.

"It's Davant Dianya," Ilcanth's voice called from his right.

She came out of another flap, her black wings streaming behind her and her body painted with swirling images in a kind of runic gown.

"It's an enchanted vintage, one that will help anyone who drinks it take pleasure in even the least pleasurable of situations," she said.

Without hesitation Coline reached out, took the glass, and drained it in a long gulp, insect and all. Ilcanth laughed, the sound like the tinkling of bells. Inside his spark flared, and he kept his eyes forward as she walked around him.

Do what you must, your wife needs you.

Ilcanth's fingers traced across the fabric at his shoulders and he flinched, but a cool feeling seeped from his stomach and calmed his breathing. His spark, hot and pulsing, evened out to a slow burn and he closed his eyes.

"This robe will not suit you for my purpose," she whispered.

Her hands moved, her words slithering into his mind and pulling strings about his limbs like a child's puppet. She pulled the robe from his freckled shoulders and the pale tone of skin shone in the brazier's light.

"You are strong," she said.

She continued to circle him, her words moving from right to front, left and behind as her touch followed the voice, each revolution going a bit slower until it traced along the tie at his waist.

"Are you feeling the potion?" she asked.

"Yes," he replied.

Her hand slipped beneath the knot, fingers moving over a tangle of hair until they slipped smooth and warm over his semi-hardness. At her touch he sprang full to life and his hands balled into fists.

"Lord Fleetwood, your height isn't the only thing over-large about you," she mocked.

"I hope that pleases you," he hissed.

She laughed, his pulse moving him in her hand as she slowly stroked along his length.

"Size can be utilized, but it is far down the list of a woman's desires," she said.

He shivered at one of her long strokes, saying, "We shall see."

"You do know what a woman wants, yes?" she asked.

His head swam, the cool vapors rising from his stomach making it harder and harder to concentrate.

"Depth, and force to feel it," he answered.

Laughter broke out again, and she withdrew her hand from him. He opened his eyes and she moved away, wings flaring once before she reached the edge of the bed and turned.

"Come here," she said.

He walked to her, looking down and she opened her wings, violet markings glowing along their surface until she floated up to meet his gaze, her toes nearly two feet off the floor. Wrapping her arms around his neck, she whispered in his ear.

"Remember this, a man shaved is a man with a purpose, and you will kiss me, every curve, starting first with my mouth. The night is long, and I promise you will know pleasure before it is done, but it won't be quick. Remember, it should never be quick."

He nodded and she drew her lips to his, the spark inside his chest fighting against the potion's cold as he wrapped his arms around her waist.

Banished Gods, what things a man must know...

He lay in the sheets, eyes wide and sweat sticky on his skin. Ilcanth lay against him, head held by his arm and one of her wings covering the bulk of his lower half. It was warm and twitched against his skin and he ran a calloused finger over the edge as he lay awake.

A dozen? Two dozen? I lost count of her shuddering pleasure during the night. She used me like an animal, my tongue aching in my mouth, and her words of instruction burned into my mind.

Lightly, always lightly until I tell you otherwise...

Slow down, and when you finally think you understand the meaning of slow, slow down some more...

Nipples aren't grapes to be plucked, leave them to the last and then you may play...

Thighs are portals, and what lies between must be tended...

Search the folds with your tongue, when you find the button, you've made it...

Suck and lick at the same time...

Each word repeated in his mind, every scene of the night's endeavor playing out across his vision until his arousal pulsed anew.

She granted me only a single release, my seed spent across the sheets by my own hand as she watched and laughed...

His spark lit anew, the frigid clouds of the potion having spent themselves in the hours between and now his heat bloomed full in his breast. Atop him, she stirred, her wings flexing.

I'll not be made a dog to be trained! I may have taken this bargain, but she has not caged me, nor shall she reap reward without some payment of her own. I am a man, a Fleetwood, and by the Banished Gods I'll show he what it is to make a deal with my bloodline.

Reaching out, he grabbed her wrist and her wing shot out full and violet as she opened her eyes.

"What is this?" she asked.

"Our bargain was for me to share your bed, not to be your slave, so I intend to share it."

Her eyes grew wide and she tried to free herself from his grasp, but he held her, rolled her over as his length jumped and played in the open air.

She shook her head, tried to press her knees together as her wings flapped against the bed but he held her down and forced her legs apart.

A cry escaped her lips as he entered her, the passions of the night still lingering as she was wet and warm.

He forced himself further inside and she cried out again, but his angle was off and he released her hands so he could move up. Once free, Ilcanth reached up and clawed his chest, pain welling from his flesh as he returned her attack with violent thrusts of his own. Her wings beat against his sides, and she pushed away with her palms but he crushed her into the bed, ground her down, and grunted with primal furry, one, two, three times and more until he released into her. His body shook, muscles locking in place as he felt half a dozen waves shiver from his shaft, the passion bleeding away with each one.

Blinking, he shook his head, sweat falling from his chin to as he looked down. Ilcanth stared up at him, eyes blazing and rimmed with green fire.

A laugh tore from her throat, and whatever unearthly beauty she possessed fled on black wings as she mocked him with her joy.

"Thank you for fulfilling your bargain, my Lord, I feared you might take a noble path after all and withhold my final victory," she cackled.

He pulled away, the laughter following him as he dropped off the edge of the bed and fell back onto the carpeted floor. On the bed Ilcanth rose up, wings aflame and a demonic mask stretching across her features.

"You payment is fulfilled, fool, coward, and rapist, so I grant you release to go to the city if that is your choosing. Remember, you must stay connected to those you enter with or you will lose them. Take the vials I've placed for you in the entry, and remember my gifts to you as they most assuredly will be needed inside the gates, for no man of honor may survive there, and so you should thrive!" she hissed.

He crawled backwards, grabbed his robe and fled the chamber, her laughter burning his back until he made it to the entry and found the needle-toothed servant waiting there.

"I see you have fulfilled your service," the man said.

Colin pulled the robe about him, saying, "Where are the vials?"

The servant provided a white smile and produced a box from within his long coat. Colin took it and left, the night air crisp and the east painted with the pink lights of the coming dawn.

Once he was away from the tent he fell to a knee and vomited, each wretch splattering the grey sand with black fluid that hissed and spat. On the third heave something struck his teeth, twitched against his tongue and he spat it out. A black insect hit the sand, eight legs twitching as it tried to right itself.

He struck down with a fist and smashed it, red essence painting a starburst around the impact.

What have I done?

His shoulders shook and he wiped the black bile from his lips as he fell back and closed his eyes.

Caroline, I'm sorry. I've come to find you and in turn have lost myself.

He wiped back tears from the corners of his eyes until his breathing came under control, and the first of the sun's rays struck the top of the tents and lessoned the green glow of the city towering above.

I may have failed you as a husband, but I will not fail in my mission. I will find you, deliver you back to the lands of your father, and there you can best decide what is to be done with me.

Beside him a thump sounded, his clothing and equipment tossed into the sand. The voice of the manservant mocked him as it departed, "Best not forget these, it's sure to be cold in the city."

He reached out, took the bundle, and stood. Taking a long breath he clothed himself and moved off to find the others, his shoulders slumped and his head bowed.

The hammer fell, each strike echoing like the call of doom as the party stood before the open gate. Green fire illuminated their visage and made shadows that danced like twisted demons behind them. Beside the small company slaves were being bound to a great iron chain, and a demon worked an anvil to forge more links to the chain as it was fed into the gate.

"I wonder why the chain doesn't come back out?" Thorn asked.

"Because there is no return from the Burning City," Roma replied.

Colin stared at the gates, his face grim and his helm drawn down tight and strapped to his head.

"You believe the slavers?" Thorn asked.

The Wizard nodded, "Why shouldn't I? Their words ring the same as any legend I've ever read concerning this place, and those were many. I chose this assignment before I journeyed to Western Gariny because the city intrigued me, and now that I am here I question my reasoning on that subject."

Thorn shook his head, "If no one leaves, then why are we going in?"

"Because nothing is for certain, and because our wives are in there," Colin said. "Still, I'll not ask you to come on this fool's errand. You've helped us this far, and that is more than enough service."

Colin turned, looked his oldest friend in the eye, "Go home to your family, be free of this curse, and feel no burden that you somehow abandoned me."

Thorn looked first at Luur, the Lowl folding his ears back on his head, saying, "There is nothing for me out here, and I think a fight will do my fiery blood good."

"I've made a vow for my people, and I'll see it through, even if it is the sacrifice of my life in that service," Dula added.

Thorn shook his head and Colin reached out to place a hand on his shoulder, "Go, this is not your fight."

"No... I'll not leave now, not after coming all this way. Besides I'd never make it out of the wastes alone anyway," Thorn said.

"Take a Mountainback. With your skills as a scout you can head east and get to the Lupin Hills in three days," Colin said.

Thorn met his eyes and smiled, "My friend, I know you mean well, but take my offer, as I fear you're going to need me."

Colin nodded, "Very well. I'll not forget this sacrifice on my account."

They turned back to the burning gate, Colin drawing forth a vial, as did the rest of them.

"There were two warnings given by the succubus. First, these potions we paid so dearly for are required to survive once you enter the city. Two, when we pass the gate we must all be connected," Colin said.

"Then we drink, hold hands, and enter?" Luur asked.

Colin nodded, and pressed the vial to his lips taking it all down in a single gulp. It burned on the way down, and he shuddered. Beside him Luur growled deep in his throat and Dula swayed on her feet before Thorn caught her.

"I fear there were curses in that potion we've not been made aware of," she said.

"What did you expect?" Roma asked.

"Everything here has a price, and even if you pay it there are no good deeds in the doing. Remember that when we get inside, because I'm sure whatever lurks there will give us no quarter," Colin said.

They nodded, and he dropped the vial before taking Thorn and Roma by the hand. Dula and Luur followed suit until they were all connected. Slowly, they all marched forward, their feet kicking up grey sand as they went.

Slaves watched them, a few calling for help and others screaming for them to go back, but they kept on moving – hands firmly clasped – until the green fire engulfed them and the world turned to emerald.

PART TWO

CHAPTER ONE

SHAY

There is time in your life where you have to transition from being the cared for to the care giver, or at least a soul responsible for yourself.

I've reached that point now, my world tilted on its axis and everything I once knew falling away as I cling to life on the precipice. Colin isn't coming for me, or if he is then it is irrelevant, as countless years will pass before he catches up with me here.

Thirty-seven years. If he's two or three days behind me, then at the minimum I'll still be alone for a century. Whatever I once was will be no more by that time, not in this place.

Still, Nowin is here, somewhere, and I made her a promise, just as I did my husband, and no matter what they take from me I'll not break. Otherwise I'm truly lost and death might as well take me.

For me, survival lies in Shay, because Shay has not baggage or preconception. She was born in this place, and so I must become her, locking away Caroline in a safe place until the time comes when she can see the light again… if that ever happens.

Shay lay on a divan, Ixis next to her and the water wall dribbling its subtle music in the background.

Another week had slipped past, Ixis continuing her instruction in pleasure, body movement, and the nuances of dressing for the position she'd assume.

"We need to discuss payment," Ixis said.

Shay turned, a sigh passing her lips, "I'm tired, must we?"

"You have only a week left before you enter the Sanctuary, so yes, we must."

"Very well," Shay yawned.

Watching her, Ixis narrowed her eyes.

"You are different these past days, and an attitude is about you that gives me hope," her teacher said.

"That is Shay," she answered and Ixis laughed and shook her head.

Standing, her golden friend smoothed the translucent silk of her shift and began to pace. Shay watched her, a slight frown alighting on her face.

"The City runs on vials, it is the only currency," she said.

"Vials?" Shay asked.

"Yes, vials. They are crystal containers laced with magic by the Writ Archons. If a person of the city dies, a piece of their soul is stripped away and locked inside the closest vial to them."

"A piece?"

Ixis nodded, "Yes, a person's soul is like an onion. It has many layers, the outer layers the largest, but the inner one the most potent. In the City, death isn't an end, not until your last layer is consumed by a vial. Depending on your will, you can live many lives here, but with each death you are still diminished, those that have lost the most layers turning grey and cold."

"Do I get a vial?" Shay asked.

Ixis laughed, "What would a lady of the Apothecary do with a vial?"

"If I kill someone I'd need it."

Ixis held up a hand, "We don't kill people here. In fact, no weapons are even allowed on Apothecary grounds. If violence is perpetrated here with a weapon the Faux Cabal would descend like a swarm of locusts and the city know this."

Shay shook her head, started to speak, but then stopped.

Too many questions. Just let her speak. You don't need to know everything today.

Ixis continued, "Those who come to the Apothecary and partake of our service provide vials to Alanthria and in turn she lets bits of that wealth come to her ladies. If you do your job well, you'll get the benefit of that wealth, and with it you can buy yourself the finer things the city has to offer."

"I've seen nothing in the city I would consider fine or that I would desire," Shay said.

"There are fantastic places beyond the Dead Gate, Shay, wonders you couldn't possibly understand, and then there is a style of living within these walls that needs to be maintained."

Ixis motioned to the room and then herself, "Do you think all you see here was given over willingly? No, I earned this chamber, these decorations and even this golden skin, and I tell you it was no small task. Once you go to the Sanctuary, you will be given over to your own keeping, my chamber denied to you, and then the tests will begin in earnest."

Shay looked around the room, then at Ixis, the woman beautiful and alien before her.

I see no appeal in what you've accomplished, but play by the rules I must, so I will comply and smile, just as Caroline once did with her tutors at the Imperial Academy.

"Where will I go then once I'm done here?" Shay asked.

Ixis sat on the divan, placed a hand on Shay's leg and provided a smile, "You will be provided a common room with the other newcomers from various Gates. I will still see you, but until you advance in the strata of our sisterhood, contact will be forbidden. For Alanthria, it is either sink or swim, and no favors will be provided."

Shay nodded, "I will be ready."

"I like to hear it, and I must say I've been impressed with your attitude this past week," Ixis said.

I've found a mask, but if that pleases you, then all the better.

"I've accepted my place, and your teaching has been invaluable," she said through that mask.

Ixis leaned forward and kissed her, their sparks mingling a moment, the connection between them having become comfortable. After the contact, she leaned back and touched Shay's chin, saying, "I will do everything I can to see you succeed. Our women are few here, but I know you have the spirit to make it."

Shay tilted her head, "Our women? I've seen many Humans here."

Ixis shook her head, "No, you've seen many females. Humans are rare as we only come through the Dead Gate, and our deliveries are slow. Most lack the will to survive the Apothecary. It's why I remembered you and took great pains to be prepared for your arrival."

"Where do these other women come from?"

"The other three Gates, but most come from Oliphras. That is the world beyond the Skull Gate," Ixis answered.

Now I begin to understand. In the Nameless Realms Humans are powerful – they command armies and lead universities. Here, our sparks are insignificant, our wealth meaningless, and what physical strength we posses undone. To the Burning City we are the lowest rung, our value only calculated as empty vessels for the pleasure of the vicious and brutal rulers of this place.

Let them think me powerless, but as long as my talkative friend gives answers, I can work to solve the puzzles of this place before they can destroy me...

"But I thought our world was closed? It's the whole reason there are no gods left," Shay said.

"It is, but this place is like a way station. All souls that come here don't ever go back. The Gates move only one way. In that case you can leave our world, just like those others who come here, but the curse doesn't allow us to return."

"How do you know that?"

Ixis shrugged, "When you've been here as long as I have, you pick things up, mostly from high ranking clients in the Sanctuary."

"But they could be lying, simply telling you there is no such way so that you won't even try," Shay argued.

"Maybe, but I'm not going to march up to the Dead Gate and try it. If it was so easy to leave, the gangs would simply abandon the city, as the single gatekeepers would be quickly overwhelmed by sheer numbers, if they even cared to stop them."

Shay didn't reply and Ixis continued on, "But let's return to the vials. To get them you must not only find, but please customers. Alanthria collects all the vials you've gained at this pursuit, and when you have repaid her service for taking you in, she will release you to your own accounts and you can starting working as you will, assuming you continue to line her coffers with vials, from which she takes a percentage.

"Still, with your mind, I don't think that will take longer than a few years to collect enough vials from the plebes to repay your debt."

"Years?" Shay asked.

Her voice was high and the spark in her chest raged. Ixis drew close, placed a hand on hers, but Shay withdrew it and Ixis sighed, "It will go quickly. Everything in this city does even if it is actually immortality you play at. I've heard people often say – if they have nothing to do, nothing required of them – that time slips past and they wonder how they ever got anything done before all the freedom found them."

"That sounds like an Aspara talking." Shay said.

"Whatever the case, this will pass, and when it does you can begin to build a fine life here, perhaps even attaining my status among the ladies."

Shay looked at her, the woman's smile genuine. Her sincerity only made the bile in her stomach churn all the more.

You are a fool! A kind fool certainly, and I'll not forget your help, but this will not be my fate.

"Do you really believe so?" Shay asked.

Ixis smiled, "Of course, otherwise I would never have told Alanthria about you."

Which will be your mistake, I fear.

"Well then, I'd better learn as much as I can before I lose your instruction. But one more question, if I may?" Shay asked.

"Anything," Ixis said.

"What about now?"

Ixis shook her head, "I'm sorry?"

"I mean, what about now? Can I have what I want now since I'm technically still under your care by way of Alanthria?" Shay asked.

Ixis stood a moment, tried to speak, stopped, touched a finger to her lips, squinted, tried to speak again, and then finally sighed without a reply.

"It's ok, I think that answers my question," Shay said. "We can move on."

Ixis nodded, smiled, and started pacing once more before she continued.

"Now, as we have vials and payment out of the way, let's continue concerning the art of the dance..."

Shay walked behind Ixis, her teacher carrying a thin chain of silver draped over her golden shoulder that led to a collar about Shay's neck.

It never becomes a slave to hold the chain of another, and yet it seems to please her.

Around them, ladies of a dozen metallic hues and even a few with more chromatic coloring lounged and ate, Lungins scampering around them as they discarded unwanted food on the floor like barbarian lords. Languages were plentiful, several women calling out to Ixis in strange tongues that she answered in kind as they passed.

The hall was long and set with an extended arch, the round doors here all doubled and painted soft copper with silvered handles and scrollwork. Violet lamps lit the lofts above, and as Ixis walked onward, a stair lifted its polished marble steps up to another level of the great house.

As they came close, Ixis pulled Shay forward, whispering, "These are the observation walks, a place where the upper caste can select perspective clients before making their way into the Sanctuary."

Shay nodded, both of them moving up the steps as two other women, both with silvered skin, moved down past them with curt nods at Ixis. Once they reached the top, there was a great circular chamber, with open arches leading out from it like the spokes of a giant wheel.

Ixis pointed, "The three halls you see before you are those of the greater Sanctuary, the place where you will make your mark on this sisterhood. The two halls on either side lead to the more secluded Deep Sanctums, a place where the upper ladies ply their trade. I suggest you spend time above the Sanctums, there is much to be learned by watching your sisters, and it's how I advanced as quickly as I have."

Shay nodded, and Ixis moved on, her course set for the central hall. When they entered it, Shay sucked in a breath. The size of the chamber was like that of a legendary Kin vault. It was a huge dome, two other planks resembling the one she was on stretching out at angles on either side. Some kind of smoky glass walls covered the other planks and didn't allow her eyes to penetrate.

She could see the same framed glass shielded the central plank as well, the glass angled out to allow a walker to look down onto the floor below, assumedly concealing their presence like the glass of the other walks.

The main floor, a mosaic of multi-colored marble blocks, was covered with mats and pillows, smoking hookah, sheltering screens, and plates of bright and steaming food. Among these were bodies, thousands of them all engaged in some kind of debaucherous revelry or more common sexual acts.

Shay raised a hand to her lips, her fingers trembling.

Beside her, Ixis whispered, "I remember the first time I saw the Sanctuary, but nothing compares to the first time you're actually down there."

"I don't think I can." Shay whispered.

Moans and laughter slithered up onto the plank, and the lewd happenings drew her eye, one after the other more unreal and bizarre than the next.

"You must, or you will perish. There is no trying at the Apothecary, and when you do what we do you have to be sure the patrons believe you enjoy every moment of it."

Shay shook her head, "Can we go?"

"No, you will stay," Ixis said. Her keeper took the tether and attached it to the rail of the walkway, then stepped back down toward the entry. "I'll be back in a few hours… the more you watch, the less it will affect you."

Shay watched Ixis leave and then looked back, the world spilling out under her in vivid detail. After a time she found a rhythm to it, a cycle of

women who came and left, of men who did their business and departed
to the far side of the chamber, and Lungins who crept about with buckets, mops, and towels.

The small creatures replaced the food, fluffed the cushions, and
made ready every detail for the copulations to come. She focused on
them, saw how they communicated with intricate hand signals while
on the floor, and how those with sloped ears tinged in red instructed
the up-facing, blue-tipped eared ones on where to do the next business.

*There are games inside games, and this place is run more fluidly than
any royal house in Nextyaria.*

Among the torrid throng she picked out men who stayed, some demanding more than one woman, and others basking like kings amid
the cushions and finery. They all held the same look: strong, cat-like,
and ready, with battle-scars covering their flesh, some pink and others
dusted to grey.

*They are fighters all, and those that lurk around them are the same only
with lower stature.*

Touching the tether, she slid it along the rail, her bare feet playing
against the wood of the plank as she kept moving forward, eyes always
watching the work below. She avoided the acts themselves, but the
conversations and actions after the couplings caused her to pause, each
movement by the participants taken in.

*There is discussion, but it is one-sided, as is the nature of the acts them-
selves. The ladies are there to make the moments a pleasure for those with
payment.*

Between the stalls, women in violet walked. They were few in number, but no man approached them and occasionally they would halt a
disheveled woman travelling back from her work on the floor and point
her to an exit beyond the left side of the half-circle.

*They monitor the floor and keep the ladies on task as well as keeping
track of how much one can take.*

When she reached the end of the plank she turned, each of the other
observation planks continuing on to the far wall, but in front of her
plank there was an open gap. Beyond it, a enormous sphere of violet
glass hung, lights inside glowing slightly and a figure could be seen
slowly walking back and forth behind the glass.

Shay watched the movement a long time before the figure stopped,
one hand waving before the glass turned transparent and Alanthria
stood in all her glory inside the sphere.

They stared at each other a moment, Alanthria smiling before looking down into the mix of flesh below.

There, amid the throng a new procession of men made their way to a half circle of divans and pillows stretching out around Alanthria's raised chamber. These men wore miss-matched armor but no weapons, their faces clean but with necks and hair still dirty.

They've come from the streets, and have forgone the bath house.

Among them stood a man tall and lean with a shaven head that bore so many tattoos they could have been mistaken for a thick-mane. His armor held metal, but for the most part was leather and mobile, and his eyes were dark-shaded as he drew up behind his men.

Several ladies of the half-circle rose and pranced about the newcomers, the men lured away one by one until the central figure was alone. His eyes watched those that remained amid the divans before he took a seat and waved off all the women that remained dancing around him.

Shay looked up, Alanthria watching her with a face like an unreadable mask until she finally tilted her head slightly and waved again, the sphere growing dark and impenetrable.

"You've made is a long way," Ixis said.

Shay jumped, and Ixis laughed, the woman coming to stand at the rail next to her.

"Sorry, I guess I was otherwise engaged," Shay said.

"The Sanctuary can do that to you," Ixis said.

Shay turned back, the leader of the newcomers still seated as new women appeared, these colored, wrapped in fine and revealing clothes, and dripping with glittering jewels. They danced for him, crawled on the floor like animals, opened themselves, and even played with each other but the man stared on, his dark eyes uncaring.

"Who is that?" Shay asked.

Ixis raised a brow, "That is Vanguard, a Human like us, and leader of the Dirk Mongers."

"Why does he just sit?"

"No one knows, but he's done that since I've been here. Each ninth day, probably for more than a century he has come with his men and has never partaken of a woman." Ixis answered.

"What is a Dirk Monger?" Shay asked.

"One of the street gangs, the blood-letters and first rung of the vial collectors. They war among the ruins and harvest vials from one another, always keeping each other in check so that the upper-echelon of the city can deal with each other exclusively and not have to worry about the common folk."

"Where do the upper echelon-type patrons go when they come to the Apothecary?"

Ixis laughed and pressed a hand on Shay's shoulder, "They are attended by better than we. The Vix Sisterhood deals with them, and only the very best of us can ever dream of moving into those ranks."

Shay kept staring at Vanguard, the man finally waving away all comers before he sat back and took a drink from a waiting Lungin.

"Come, we should go," Ixis said.

"A moment, I've not finished yet," Shay said.

Ixis withdrew her hand, saying, "Very well, as this is a much needed teaching lesson, but don't take too long, I still have my other duties to perform. I will wait in the gallery below."

Shay nodded, her hands twining on the rail.

He is young. The tattoos make him older in appearance and the armor pads just the right angles to give him breadth.

Vanguard took another drink, then placed the glass gently back on the tray, the Lungin nearly dropping it in the process.

He knows common manners, but the hold he had on the glass is no noble-trained grip, so he at least chooses to act the part. He keeps himself from sin, which means, like me, something outside this place must matter to him.

She closed her eyes, Vanguard's face rising up before her. She stripped away the tattoos, grew hair upon his head, and presented him in plain clothes.

A commoner like the rest of these poor souls, and if I'm right he's a coastal man, probably the shores of Gariny proper.

Opening her eyes, she stole one last look at the warrior as he lounged in the cushions, and then ran back along the rail, the silver cord trailing behind her.

CHAPTER TWO

SHAY

Information, my tutors at the Academy used to say, is the key to opening all locks. In this case I'd apply the word "shackles," but the principle is the same.

My time is limited, every hour that passes puts me closer to what I witness in the Sanctuary and I have to understand everything I can of this hell before I'm thrown into it.

For this I need Ixis, and she's not one to hold her tongue when asked a question, or simply stop talking at any particular point during the day. I have to use this to my advantage, mold the conversation, and find the answers hidden inside her words that even she herself might not know.

Whatever has gone before I must bury deep, the aftershocks may still shiver my flesh and turn my stomach, but survival is based on moving forward and never looking back.

The true question concerning this revelation is that if I don't look back, will I lose the good that is behind me as well as the bad? In this case, I'm very afraid of the answer. But nonetheless, I am Shay, and Shay will have answers.

Shay made a spinning move but Ixis stepped forward and stopped her as three Lungins ceased their music. The three little creatures had strange instruments, part drum and part lute, their deft little hands going from stings to leather drumhead without a pause as they made a torrid and lilting music.

"No, you'll catch no clients with moves like that. You have to forget the teachings you've learned in our realm, what I'm trying to teach you is about movement, not moves," Ixis said.

Shay nodded, sweat upon her brow and her hair sticking to the sides of her face. She was naked save for a silk scarf that bound her breasts and two lengths of fabric supported by a chain about her waist that concealed some of her privates, at least until she moved.

"I will try again," Shay said.

Ixis shook her head, "No, you're too tired now, and you've gotten progressively worse this past hour. Have a seat and take a rest."

Shay sat upon a stool in one corner, the Lungins waived from the room and Ixis practicing a few moves against one mirrored wall as she watched. After several minutes and two full glasses of water, Shay spoke, "I've got a question."

Ixis turned, but kept dancing, "Yes?"

"If you are correct, and thirty-seven years passes inside the Burning City to every day that passes outside, then how long would a twenty second difference be between entries?"

"Three days," Ixis replied.

Shay raised her eyebrows, "Really?"

"Yes."

"That is quick math," Shay said.

"No, I just knew what you were really asking. There is a three day interval between entries from the Dead Gate. That means that the other slaves brought in on the constantly moving chain, each twenty seconds removed, reach the city every three days. I didn't do the math, I just know the outcome," Ixis answered.

Nowin, you've been here three more days than I, and I hope you've found the world more to your liking than I have.

"Who was she, a maid servant?" Ixis asked.

"No, she was a friend, the wife of my hus..." Shay trailed off.

Ixis turned around, a wan smile on her face, "You can make those mistakes with me, just don't do it with a client or Alanthria."

Shay nodded and Ixis continued, "And if you want to know, the answer is no, we've received no other women in the past weeks from the Dead Gate, so this friend of yours was taken someplace else, probably into the gang ranks."

"Do the gangs have women?" Shay asked.

"Yes, but you'll not see them here, unless of course they have a taste for women as well. Some female newcomers are taken as pleasure slaves in the most successful of gangs, but considering the true prize is to come here, that doesn't happen often. Instead, they'll become fighters like the rest."

"But I haven't seen women here," Shay said.

"No, you wouldn't. Female gangers don't come to the Sanctuary or the Sanctums, instead they go to the River Gallery where the Kapa are kept."

"Kapa?"

Ixis nodded, "The male pleasure slaves. Soon, you'll get to know them as well, but those of the lower ranks don't mix, so unless you are a Lady of the East or West Sanctum, you'll not see a Kapa. Still, when you do get to have a Kapa, it is worth the wait as they are as experienced in giving pleasure as we are."

Shay sat a moment, Ixis moving to the far wall and taking down a towel to dry her face.

"Are you a Lady of the East or West Sanctum?" Shay asked.

"The East, but soon I will be of the West, and then my life will change again."

"What is the difference?" Shay asked.

"The Ladies of the East have taken their first step into the upper ranks of the Apothecary, and once they've attained the wealth required from clients, they move up to the West, where more rights are at hand and you can slowly find a place outside the Sanctuary to build a career."

"Then there is a way out?" Shay asked.

Ixis nodded, "Yes, but don't dream so big yet. There are many and many again years between you and a floor administrator or the like."

Shay sighed, and Ixis patted her on the shoulder, "Come, we'll take a lunch, and then I must be away to other duties."

The two left the instruction room, Ixis attaching a light chain to a collar around Shay's neck before they moved out into the hall.

The meal was resplendent, a fine collection of spiced meats, fried tubers, and steamed vegetables. Shay ate until her stomach hurt, diced fruit and iced cream the final delicacy to pass her lips.

Ixis sat at the table across from her with a plate partially full from disuse, her eyes staring out a window into a dark stand of trees beyond a heavy stone fence.

Taking a last bite of a dipped fruit, white with cream, Shay lay back in her chair and sighed. Ixis looked back and smiled.

"Did you enjoy it?"

"Yes, but I don't understand," Shay answered.

"Understand what?"

"Where it all comes from in a place like this?"

"Some comes from the Gates, others are grown or raised within the city. Food production is the domain of the Cloak Brotherhood. Those nature disciples keep the city self-sustaining just in case the Gates close or our imports are cut off," Ixis said.

"How many outside powers like the Cloak Brotherhood are there?" Shay asked.

Ixis picked up a wedge of fruit, dipped it in the cream, and then sucked it between her stained lips, saying, "There are eleven greater houses in the city, all of which are charged with a specific purpose that keeps the city moving along like a well-oiled machine."

"To what end?"

Ixis smiled, "Only the gods know, and yet we continue to move on."

Shay looked out the window, to the right of the dining room there was another structure that moved close to the wall and had windows facing the woods and a watercourse beyond.

"Is the Apothecary completely walled?" Shay asked.

"No, but I hope you're not thinking of escape."

"No, I realize what I must do, and there would be no place in the city for me to go anyway, I've already seen what is out there."

"It's good you understand that, and now that we've enjoyed a meal, I thought I'd give you something," Ixis said.

Her friend clapped her hands and Lungins appeared, one of them carrying a hand-tooled leather bag. Ixis took it while the plates and remaining food were cleared. Once the table was empty, she slid the pack to Shay.

"What's this?" Shay asked.

"Something that you'll be able to take with you, along with the three dresses we've already had you fitted for," Ixis said.

"I don't know that those could be rightly called dresses," Shay said.

Ixis laughed, "In the Sanctuary, they might very well be too conceal-ing."

"So I've seen."

Ixis shook her head and waved a hand, "Just open it."

Shay unwrapped the leather string that held it shut and reached in-side. Her fingers found several objects and she pulled them out to rest on the table. When the pack was empty she looked at them all arrayed before her.

There were three vials with a red liquid and a small black insect sus-pended in the fluid. Beside these a ribbon tie held several small brush-es and five small jars of brightly colored pigment. A fine silver mirror reflected her face, the image not one she readily recognized. The final piece was a small book that had a ruin-covered quill pen stuck through a leather strap that bound it.

"I don't know what to say," Shay managed.

"Every girl that enters the hall receives a gift from her trainer, and I might have gone a bit overboard but I couldn't help myself."

Shay shook her head and looked up at Ixis. The metallic-skinned woman sat and smiled at her, and she reached out to take her hand.

"I really don't know what I would have done without you," she said.

Ixis's face faltered a moment, the woman reaching up to brush a tear from the corner of one eye before she recovered her smile.

"Just make me proud," Ixis said.

Shay nodded and looked back down at the presents, whispering, "That is my intent."

"The vials are Davant Dianya, a vintage that will help you accept acts otherwise beyond your limits," Ixis said.

Shay shuddered, and Ixis continued, "Lungins will usually do your primping before you enter the Sanctuary, but if you wanted to add your own touches I've included some of my favorite personal pigments, and a mirror to see what you're doing."

"And the book?" Shay asked.

"The book is to remember."

Shay looked up, "I thought I was supposed to forget?"

"That is the duty of each of us, and probably the best thing we can do, but I heard your promise to your friend in those cages, and I know she helped get you this far."

Ixis paused, looked out the window, and then continued, "Time here loses meaning, as does most things in your life. I've found that I wish I remembered things that were once important to me, because I often find myself adrift. I thought I might save you this melancholy if I could, so a journal seemed the best way to do it. There are times when girls drift too far in the flow of time, cease their craft and are lost to us. I don't want that for you."

Shay picked up but the book and ran her hand across the tooled leather at the cover.

"It's beautiful," she said.

Ixis nodded, "Perhaps, but guard what you put in there because – although what you remember might not have taken place inside this city – there are those who might still try to use it against you. Keeping one's journey alive in writing is a double-edged sword. Never forget that."

I will do what I must, and I will protect my memories as long as I am able.

"Good, then with that out of the way, let's get back to my chambers," Ixis said.

Reaching out, she attached the chain to Shay's choker and the two of them made their way from the dining solarium to the private suites, the pack of goods clutched tightly to Shay's chest.

CHAPTER THREE

SHAY

What happens daily to the women in the Sanctuary can't be me. I simply won't let that happen. There are things people are capable of and things they aren't, and sometimes you can straddle the distance, but in this case I'm not to that point.

I'd rather die than spend years as a whore, no matter the promises I've made. But one thing that was taught to me at the Academy was that if you ever wanted to succeed in life you needed to challenge the rules.

This is what I've determined to do. The Apothecary works on a system of rules, but the people brought here are all victims, their minds barely hanging on as is, and they can only think of the next day, not the future as a whole.

I, Shay, refuse to be a victim, and if I'm my father's daughter, then I will find a way, just like he did during the Five Year War, because this too is a war, and the prize is my soul.

Ixis slipped from the room, the lights dim and the bed still warm where she'd slept next to Shay. Minutes passed, Shay breathing steadily until she was certain her instructor was gone.

The Sanctuary calls, my sister, and you must ever be its slave.

She rose from the bed, removed the chain from her choker, and made her way to the door. The hall outside was empty save for a few scurrying Lungins, the creatures a focal point for her during the past week as she'd spent time on the viewing planks.

Down the hall, pass three ruby doors, left at the junction, two pale-green doors, and then you're there.

Her bare feet made no sound as she slipped out, back straight and eyes forward.

Keep up appearances, only a sulking slave should draw attention, not one that looks to have a purpose. She was a noble. She knew how to walk with the confidence of authority.

She kept a steady pace, passed a lounging lady on a divan that paid her no mind, and made it to the junction. Two more women spoke there, but they turned away from her, their whispers growing lower as she walked past.

More doors and another long hall played out before she made it to the amber door, the scrollwork heavier and more pronounced around the portal.

She reached up a trembling hand, took the knob and twisted. The door opened, the room within well-lit and large, several Lungins stirring from places where they slept on the floor.

The little creatures hissed and barked in their strange language, but Shay held up a hand, made two quick gestures, and the Lungins lowered their ears and backed away.

I've studied your hand signals, I know the threats of your over-bosses.

Three large arachnid spinners hung from the ceiling to one side of the room, a dozen buckets below each of them. Their long brown legs were drawn up around their segmented bodies and she approached them with her head bowed.

Yes.....

She stopped, looked back at the door, but no one was there.

Yes....

Inside her mind, something slithered like a worm between her brain and her skull. She grabbed either side of her head, a flash of pain blinding her before it quickly faded.

Yes....

She looked up, one of the spinners dropping down to its buckets, legs blooming out around it as runes flared along the limbs.

"I need a dress," she said.

Yes....

The worms crawled again, but the pain was gone, only the odd feeling of discomfort. Two of the creature's legs reached beneath its abdomen, a length of silk coming forth as it brought it forward and began spinning. The tips of its legs glowed as it worked, the silk congealing into full fabric that was then dipped in the pigment buckets before finally being attached by the upper legs as the shape of a dress started to appear.

A Lungins came forward, offered her a drink, and she took it, another brought out a padded stool and she sat, the creatures bowing and hissing around her as she watched the magic being worked before her.

The dress took form, the color a honeyed white, the bell of the skirt wide, and the top cut across the shoulder. It was a plain thing, simple and purposeful, without any hint of the semi-clothing the ladies of the house wore.

Lungins purred as they sat with her, watching, a delicate scrollwork beginning to be embroidered on the fabric. A swirling pattern like wind bound into visual reality spilled across the material, and here and there delicate yellow flowers were sown.

Shay smiled, the spinner reading her every thought, the dress a thing of a peasant's dreams.

I remember my days in my father's hall, and how he'd let me play with the commoners and attend their marriage festivals.

Within minutes the full dress hung from the upper legs, the spinner leaning out and offering it to Shay.

She stood, reached up and took it.

Yes...

"Yes indeed," she replied.

The spinner withdrew and climbed its tether to rejoin its two sisters, the Lungins yipping happily around Shay's legs.

She took the dress, folded it, and left the room, Lungins hissing as she closed the door. The hall was no longer empty, several women moving along the length. Shay straightened, held the dress like an important parcel, and joined them as they walked.

"The Gutter Scabs are in tonight," one said.

"A wicked score that, but at least Lazarus is with them, so a true win is possible," another comment.

"And Cain, I heard he dropped a quarter vial last 10th day on Kayla," the first said.

"Kayla is a whore among whores, we could all be so lucky," a third said.

"It's easier for a Pagras, their world is twisted to begin with," the second said.

"Well, at least you're not Human," the first added.

The trio laughed, their course passing the junction and Shay broke away to the right. She half-ran up the hall, found Ixis's door and slipped inside.

Her exhale broke the silence of the room, eyes closing as she leaned back against the door.

Banished Gods, thank you for this deliverance.

She moved back into the room, found her leather pack which held the bits of fabric that made up her gifted Sanctuary dresses and the few other preening implements Ixis had provided her and slid the dress inside.

When the pack was secure, she slid back into bed and closed her eyes.

One more day and you join the other women. Then the dominion of Shay truly begins…

She clutched her pack to her chest, Ixis next to her and a collection of other women around them, each with an upper lady at their side.

"You will remember what I taught you, yes?" Ixis asked.

Shay nodded, turned to say something but the double door opened and a tall woman with the same violet skin as Alanthria came out. She surveyed those gathered, her mouth firm and a hand slowly sliding two fingers back and forth against one another.

The tall newcomer asked a question.

As one, the upper ladies replied in a language Shay didn't understand, other than a title, 'Vanca'

Vanca nodded, her hand going out to wave the collection inside as she said something foreign three times before Shay understood. "Come, we have preparations to make as I want you on the floor by 8th Day."

Shay's stomach fell, but she went with the other girls, all of them hollow-eyed save two who stood close to each other and whispered something as they entered the door.

The room beyond was a circle, burnished bronze doors stood around the circumference, Vanca heading to one along the right curve. Vanca continued speaking, repeated it again in another three languages before finally switching to the Garin Trade Tongue.

"You are fifth door girls if anyone asks, and I am Vanca, your ward."

Vanca opened the fifth door, a short hall behind leading to another circle room with pallets on the floor that pressed against the walls, a single shelf at the head of each. A candle sat on the top of the shelf and a folded blanket and padded wooden block were beside it.

Vanca spoke again, the trade tongue her third choice this time, "Take one of the pallets, it doesn't matter which."

Shay went for one but another girl bumped her out of the way. She adjusted course, but missed another. Finally, she had to turn back, the only pallet remaining on the left side of the door. Vanca stood next to it, a frown on her face.

"Indecision will kill you just as fast as letting another girl take what you want," she said.

One of the bright-eyed women said something in a foreign tongue and Vanca replied in kind, the room settling down. She spoke again, addressing them all with Shay being the last she turned to.

"I hate repeating myself, especially for an inept Human, so you'd better learn Oliphras or Pagras if you want to understand what's going on."

Shay nodded, Vanca watching her a long moment before she shook her head and moved to the door.

Ixis... why didn't you tell me there was a language issue, and why did the women in the halls speak the common tongue?

Vanca called something twice over her shoulder, and then exited, Shay standing with her pack in her hands as the other women got settled in.

The girl on the pallet next to her reached over and took her blanket as she stood watching the door.

"Hey!" Shay said.

The girl didn't seem to hear her, and the girl beyond the thief started laughing. Shay marched over and grabbed the blanket back, pulling the girl to her feet in the process. They stood eye to eye a moment, the laughing girl calling out to the others in her foreign tongue.

"This blanket is mine," Shay said.

The girl spat something she didn't understand and reached for the blanket. Shay brought her forehead down in a quick strike as the girl leaned in for her grab. She saw stars, and blood splattered her cheeks as she shattered the girl's nose.

The thief screamed as her knees buckled, and Shay shook off the stars before she snapped out her foot and kicked the already down girl in the side of the head. A blaze of pain shot up her leg and her foot throbbed but the girl was laid out across her pallet, blood streaming from her crocked and swelling nose and her left leg twitching in a unconscious spasm.

"Anyone else?" Shay screamed.

The laughing stopped, the girls going back to their business. Shay picked up the thief's blanket, heat blooming from her, and wiped the woman's blood from her face before throwing it back on her. From a small door set in the far curve of the room four Lungins appeared. The creatures ran forward, picked up the unconscious girl and carried her into their hole.

Shay watched them go, something in the pit of her stomach falling.

Banished Gods, what did I just do? Father, I remember every rough lesson you taught. You said that if you want to survive in hostile environs there is no quarter, but I fear I may have doomed that girl.

She could almost hear his reply, '*better her than you, my girl.*'

The Lungins door stayed open a moment, another creature coming out to mop up the remaining blood with a yellow sponge. When it returned from its task the door slammed shut with a hollow thump.

Shay sat down, placed her pack into the shelf and then laid out her blanket over the pallet. A now empty pallet away, the one she already thought of as "Laugher" said something.

She looked over, the girl staring at her before saying something again.

"I don't understand you," Shay said.

The girl repeated the words.

Shay shook her head and raised her hands. The girl nodded, pointed at the door, then at all the girls in the room. Shay nodded as the girl smiled and then pretended to wash herself before finally counting out six fingers very slowly.

Six hours to the bath...

"I get it, thank you," Shay said.

The girl tipped her head.

Shay nodded, smiled, and gave a slight bow. The girl returned the gesture, the violet lanterns in the room dimming as the girls settled in. Shay did the same, at first facing the abandoned mat and finally rolling away to face the door.

Sleep took her, but dreams of the bloody girl being drug from the room plagued her thoughts.

CHAPTER FOUR

SHAY

I'm alone now, no Nowin to show me strength, no Ixis to provide me knowledge. Now it is my turn, and if I'm to survive I must remember all the teachings I've had in life. My gifts were great, but I never saw them as such until now. My thanks I give anyway to my father for his dedication to me and to the Empire for demanding my service at their Academy.

There is a puzzle here, something to be solved, and I feel that in my bones. If Shay can find the answer then I'll not have to survive the Burning City, instead I'll thrive in it, even if the costs still run deep.

The baths steamed, and the girls of the Fifth Door lay among the warm water. Most were quiet but a few shared conversations as Lungins raced around the slick marble ledges attending to any need.

Shay stared off into space, submerged up to her neck, and her hair tied up on her head.

The time is coming. I can feel the tension beneath the surface, the girls knowing what comes next.

The Laugher slid close, foreign words spilling from her lips, but Shay kept staring forward until the girl moved away.

There's no reason to talk, especially if I can't understand.

She sighed, brought her hand up and splashed water on her face. The water was scented, and salt played on the tiles beneath her.

Across the pool the blue-circle door opened, Vanca entering as the girls came to attention. The violet woman spoke twice, both languages unintelligible, but the girls moved and Shay went with them.

They dried themselves and returned to the Fifth Door, each girl putting on one of the outfits tucked in their shelves.

Shay opened her pack and took out a yellow tangle of silk and ties. The thing was an impossible puzzle, and she struggled to put it on until Laugher came over , speaking quickly as she turned the tangles and managed to get the modicum of fabric covering the right places.

Laugher then stood in front of her, smiled, gave a little clap and then went back to dressing herself.

Shay drew her fingers over the straps and silk bits, her mouth dry and her knees shaky. Lungins moved into the chamber, the little creatures swarming around the girls and she was coaxed to her knees as the creatures began tugging and pinning her hair. One of them, a creature with back-drawn and green-tinged ears, stood before her and brought out a brush.

It had overlarge eyes that were blue like the ocean but alien with three dark irises. Its skin was dry and scaling around the eyes and mouth, but the rest of its flesh was a subtle grey and its fingers were overly long and held an extra knuckle.

Whispering, it hissed a few words and touched one of the dozen runes on the thin brush. The fibers at the head turned from a clean brown to vibrant yellow that twinkled in places like glittering diamonds.

The Lungin slowly closed its eyes, then opened them and nodded. She stared a moment before it repeated the action.

Close my eyes. Got it.

She complied, her eyes falling shut and the creature drew the brush across her lids. It then hissed and she reopened them as it touched another rune and the brush head turned red. It pursed its lips, and she did the same, the brush painting her again.

When it had finished, it moved off, the collection around her spilling away as she reached up to feel the bundle of hair now rising atop her head.

You can do this. Just stay in the rear, look bored, and don't draw too much attention.

Vanca finally called out, and the girls fell in line, Shay taking up a position near the back. Laugher was behind her, and she tried to relax, the girl crowding her space and whispering quick words as they marched from the room.

They moved down a long hall, passed two junctions, and then turned left to a metal oval that was split with a violet silk rope. Vanca turned to them, inspected each, and then began a short speech that was lost on Shay.

Toward the middle of the pack, a girl fainted, and Lungins quickly picked her up and ran away with her.

Laugher leaned in and said something, but Shay just took a breath and closed her eyes.

You can do this. You can do this.

Vanca said a few more words and then pulled the rope, a gong sounding somewhere and the metal door swinging in on a single great hinge.

From beyond the portal a smell of sweet perfume and heavy sweat poured out around the girls, and the sounds of voices drifting with it. A woman cried out in passion, another screamed in pain, and the laughter of men rose and fell above the rest.

Vanca spoke again, the girls marching into the Sanctuary. Shay stepped over the threshold, the chamber looking even vaster from a position on the floor, the grey walkways above seemingly lifeless and a world away in their safety.

She entered the half-circle, the area arrayed with other girls, these standing and moving through the portal as the Fifth Door entered. They passed her without a word, most dead-eyed and listless, their make-up smeared and their hair a shamble.

A hard day's work in the Sanctuary...

She took a place on a divan, three rows of girls in front of her and one to the rear. Laugher sat across from her in the second row, the girl turning back several times to give her a smile.

The great door slammed closed, the echo making Shay wince and she whispered a prayer to gods long lost to her world.

Around them the revelry in the hall continued on unabated, and occasionally a drunken patron would stumble into the circle and take a girl with him. Time passed, and Shay's stomach grew troubled as more and more girls were pulled away. She reached up and pulled bits of her hair down from the Lungin styling, ran a hand along her lips to smear the red shading across her cheek and rubbed at her eyelids. Laugher watched her, but she kept working, drawing tears from her eyes only to wipe them across the pigments.

Laugher said something, but she kept staring forward, the time slipping away slowly.

From the right of the half-circle a door was opened and men entered. These were dressed in dark clothes and wore their hair long. They walked with shoulders swaying and heads held back, their dark eyes looking only forward.

The Men of Dusk, always on the 8th day.

The men came forward and a chime sounded, the girls of the Fifth getting to their feet. A few other stragglers from the main floor that were taking a rest on the divans also stood. Shay kept her eyes forward, slumped her shoulders, and blew out her stomach, the men moving around them, some touching, others laughing at some unheard joke.

One of the men moved past her, and found Laugher. He ran a hand down the girl's back and she jumped which brought a smile to his face. He said something and Laugher shook her head.

Don't panic…

Laugher's eyes were wide and she tried to take a step away from the man but he grabbed her wrist. She threw a fist at him, but he caught it and let out a great laugh as he called to his fellows. They returned a few words as she struggled, her voice raising and her pleas more fevered.

A man near him said something and the man released her, Laugher falling away and backing from the half-circle only to have a swarm of Lungins catch her. She screamed, clawed, and bit, but they brought her down and carried her from the floor.

Shay felt bile rise in her throat, and the man who'd attempted to take Laugher shook his head and turned back to face her. A tremor tore through her and her spark flared as he approached.

He said something, but she didn't reply and she closed her eyes. After a moment his voice spoke again, and a girl behind her answered. Opening her eyes she turned around and saw another of her Fifth Door sisters that was directly behind her taking the man's hand.

A sigh escaped her lips, and the remainder of the Men of Dusk took up their choices but she remained standing along with a few other stragglers who had come in from the floor. She mimicked their manner, lay as though exhausted messaged her cheeks to keep them flushed.

The leader of the Men of Dusk sat in the center of the half-circle, Lungins attending him as he waited. He drank wine, ate fruit, and within minutes three skin-hued ladies stood before him and danced.

He watched them, eyes glazed, and finally gave a sharp whistle. A Lungin appeared and he withdrew a vial from his belt, the crystal container shimmering with golden essence. He deftly drew off the stopper and held it out. The Lungin raised a crystal goblet and the leader poured in three precise drops.

The Lungin hissed and bowed, and the leader replaced the stopper and waved one of the ladies over. She came on, provided him a hand, and they departed the half-circle. Shay craned her neck, watched them drift through the throng around them and disappear through the violet walls that flanked the floor on either side.

The Sanctums.

Lying back on the divan, she took a breath, the fire inside dwindling as the half-circle drew quiet. Hours passed, some of the Fifth drifting back. They were covered in sweat, hair mussed, and preening pigments smeared, but they took their places and waited.

Shay started counting the times a woman in a violet dress would slide past, inspect the remaining girls, but she stopped when the light inside the hall changed. She looked up, above her Alanthria's sphere had gone from violet to clear, and the woman stood atop a step and surveyed the chamber.

She started to look away, but Alanthria's eyes caught hers and there was a moment of tension before the mistress looked away and Shay took a breath.

Banished Gods, let me survive to the morrow.

A Lungin appeared, and Shay jumped, but it passed her and she closed her eyes, hands shaking.

Just one more day, that's all I need.

Somewhere a chime sounded and the massive door opened, cool clean air spilling into the hall. Beyond it a collection of girls came forward, each with flawless hair, skin, and raiment.

The girls around Shay stood and walked out, Shay following them until they all stood in the junction. A few of them departed down halls, but those of the Fifth remained, Vanca appearing within moments of the great door closing again.

The mistress moved around each girl silently until she came to Shay. She leaned forward, sniffed, and then a frown slid across her dark lips.

"You've not been with a patron this day. It happens, from time to time, but know this, if you are without the essence of a man's pleasure on the morrow, I'll have you collected. Understood?"

Shay nodded, Vanca turning away as she called to the rest. They fell in line and she led them back down the halls to the bathes, each girl peeling off her clothing before getting into the warm water.

No one spoke this time, those around Shay either wrapping arms around themselves, crying, or staring silently off into the mist.

Shay washed the pigments from her face, drew the pins from her hair, and breathed in the clean mist, the bath easing her muscles bound up by the tension of the evening's wait.

It wasn't long before Vanca appeared again, the girls standing and moving from the room after toweling their bodies.

When they at last came to the Fifth Door, Vanca said a few departing words, gave a hard look at Shay, and then closed the door.

The other girls dropped onto mats, half of which were now empty, and Shay pulled her blanket over her. She stared for a long time at the mats next to her, images of the bloody thief being carried away and Laugher struggling as she was manhandled from the Sanctuary dancing in her vision.

Sleep wasn't easy to find, but when the lights fell, she did slip into a fitful rest, dreams of men touching her waking her on more than one occasion.

CHAPTER FIVE

SHAY

My father was a prisoner once, bound and taken into the Planer Archipelago. He said it wasn't the darkest moment of his life, and I can't imagine what that horrible point might have been, but he did tell me that as he sat in his cage all he could think about were ways to escape so he could return to my mother and me.

It was what kept him going, and although he never found his own way out, he lived inside the cruelty until the time did come when others mounted the walls of his distant prison to rescue him so he could return home.

My mother speaks of it differently. She tells a tale where my father left without a word as she worked the tables of the Emerald Serpent beyond the Black Gate in Taux. He'd received word of a kingdom that was his for the taking. She thought he abandoned us both, but without proof she had to believe in what her gut told her, that he would return. For over a year she spurned the approaches of other men, worked her fingers to the bone to support us both, and when my father did come home, she stood before him with clear conscience that she'd been true.

I know not what fate holds for me, or if I will ever stand before my husband again, but even if my body is soiled, I swear to any power that will listen, even you observer, that I will have a clear conscience as to what I've done. Let Shay carry the stain so that Caroline can be free of it.

The girls broke their fast, the bulk of the remaining Fifth Door stragglers from the Sanctuary slipping into the chamber during the long night. When Vanca entered, seven of the twenty mats were still empty, but the woman didn't acknowledge the absence as she gave another unintelligible speech.

When she was done the girls lined up, Shay in the rear, and they marched off to a dance class. This was led by two hued women, and they carried long thin sticks that they used as both time counters and switches if a girl was out of position.

It was an hour of exhausting practice, all the girls sweating before Vanca returned and took them to the baths. They lounged in the water, a few talking now, but Shay kept to herself, stomach churning as the time passed within the mists.

Vanca called them forth again, brought them back to the Fifth where she led them in a series a stretches and then left them to dress.

Shay took up her pack, the tether twining around her forefinger as she unwrapped the closure and then looked inside. The dress she'd commissioned from the spinners still waited, and she drew it out, laid it on the mat and then sat down before it.

Some of the girls called to her, some laughed, but she didn't pay them a look as she closed her eyes and took strands of her hair in her hands.

A thousand times in my life I've done this, just as you did it for me when I was too young mother.

Fingers spinning, she drew the long pieces together, braiding the locks into long ropes of silky black.

When the Lungins entered, she waved them off with the hand gestures of their bosses, the diminutive creatures backing away with hisses and bows.

Once a quarter of her hair was tied back in braids, she stood and slipped on the dress. Its few ties laced at the front and were easy to bind. When she turned around, the other girls stared at her in a small gang, their near-naked bodies in direct opposition to the covering she wore.

She pressed her palms against the skirt, smoothed it down, and bowed to them. Silence reigned, and only when Vanca entered was it broken. One of the girls pointed and said something.

Vanca turned, raised one of her delicate black eyebrows and then waved the speaker off. The mistress stepped forward, towered over Shay, but she met the woman's gaze.

"What do you play at?" Vanca asked.

"I will not go another night without collecting my due," Shay said.

Vanca smiled, her eyes burning with a sudden green fire.

"Indeed." the mistress whispered.

Vanca turned in a great flurry, waved the girls on and spoke in their tongue. They fell in line, once again Shay taking up the rear.

As they marched through the halls, several of the lounging ladies sat up and watched, Shay drawing many comments as they passed. By the time they made the great junction, half a dozen ladies had collected there, all of them whispering, but Shay kept her face forward.

Just let him be there. Banished Gods, bless me on this 9th day with at least that much.

A chime rang and the door opened. The Fifth made their way into the heat and smell of the Sanctuary, the ladies that had followed their procession departing up a stair off the junction to the gangways above.

Watch all you want, and you might learn something.

They walked into the half-circle, the girls departing their work and twisting around backward to get a look at Shay as she passed.

Violet light streamed down from above, and Shay's eye adjusted to the dimness as she took a seat on a divan. When the rest of the girls lowered themselves she got a good view of the leader's platform, two hued ladies dancing there as the form of Vanguard sat eating a succulent, his eyes on a far wall.

Do it now. Don't let the opportunity pass.

She stood, walked from the lounge and up the small dais as Vanguard turned his head, his hand falling away from his mouth when he saw her.

She stopped, smiled, lowered herself in a simple curtsy as she flared out the dress. Her bare feet turned out slightly and she lifted her left arm straight out, her palm moving from the down position to the up.

Remember the girls of your youth. Remember the Spring dance...

Lightly, she took three steps to the left, tipped her head back right, and raised her right arm as she lowered her left. Her palm turned again, and she looked up at Vanguard. He was standing now, face pale as a ghost, and his hand waved away the hued ladies.

"Away!" he barked when they delayed too long.

Good, you speak my tongue. That makes this a bit easier.

He half-stumbled down the steps, the violet light from above turning gold as it lit the half-circle.

Alanthria is watching. Make it count!

Shay put both of her hands to her skirt, raised it slightly to expose her ankles and did a small series of steps with her feet, her eyes never leaving those of Vanguard as he approached.

She summoned up her best common accent, something that always made her mother's skin crawl.

"Lord and Liar, I see ya'ave a likin' for wha I offer now, so will ya dain to give a common lass a dance?" she asked.

Vanguard broke into a smile and took a step toward her proffered hand, but a Lungin quickly stepped between them, a crystal goblet raised in his hands.

The warrior looked down, reached into a pack at his side and drew out a handful of glimmering gold vials, a collective gasp rising from the women around the half-circle. Without even looking, Vanguard dropped them all into the goblet, the clank of the crystals making Shay's skin shiver.

The Lungin's eyes grew wide, and it staggered back, one hand moving up to keep the vials from spilling out, and a woman in violet appeared like a phantom, her hands brushing the Lungin away as she stepped up on the first level of the dais.

Vanguard paid the tall woman no heed as he grabbed Shay up into his arms with a great laugh and twirled her around in the air as a squeal escaped her lips.

"Master Vanguard, if you would like a private room among the Sanctums, one is waiting," the floor administrator offered.

He stopped, held Shay close as his eyes searched hers. The world stood still, and at last he spoke, "Yes, I think a private room would be perfect."

With that he spun her about until he held her like a bride before the threshold and walked behind the floor administrator as she made her way to the west Sanctum, all eyes watching them as they went.

The sheets were tangled, the screened chamber open to the planks that stretched far above and Shay lay with her head against Vanguard's naked chest. He was a big man, yet lean and still half a foot shorter than her husband, and less grand about his loins. His skin was pale, like all those of the city, and a thousand scars lay open its surface, her fingers slowly running over them as she listened to him breath.

I've yet to lay like this with my own husband, and I've enjoyed this coupling all the more than the times I spent with Colin.

Vanguard drew in a great breath and stirred, his arm sliding up her naked back before he sat up.

"I never thought I'd find you," he said.

She looked up, his amber eyes twinkling in the violet light from above.

"Was I lost and didn't realize it?" she asked.

He smiled, kissed her, and lay back down. She climbed up him, her arms crossed and resting on his chest.

This is the second man I've ever let kiss me, and I didn't mind it... Shay didn't mind it.

"It's a tough thing, living in this place," he began, "and I know you're not her, but that doesn't make it any less extraordinary to finally find you after so many years of waiting."

"And it is no less precious that I've found you," she replied.

He looked up, asking, "Then we are understood, you and I?"

"Indeed, and I will not disappoint you if you grant me the same favor," she replied.

He nodded, "Then let it be, and we will speak of it no more. I am Vanguard."

"I am Shay."

"May we partake?" he asked.

She reached down, found him ready and firm in her grasp and he sighed at her touch. The fervor of the previous coupling had roused her spark, although no release had come to her, and she was easily lit again as she found his lips.

Stroking him long, she kissed and played. Vanguard tried to rise but she remembered the ladies observed from above, so instead she pulled herself atop him. His hands ran along her hips as she slid down and let him slip inside her.

She closed her eyes, her braids falling down to cover her face as he eased in, fingers tightening on her hips as he did. Their sparks mingled, fought, and flared as sweat shown on her brow while she slowly ground into him. He kept her close, forced her down, and stayed the course until he slid a hand up to cup her breast, his calloused thumb circling and teasing her nipple.

A whimper slipped from her mouth and she bit her bottom lip, flashes of sensual magic lighting her brain. He grunted, drove his feet into the floor and lifted her. She gasped, fingers digging into his chest as he drove deep and tinges of pain washed away the ecstasy.

Vanguard's hand left her breast, grabbed her shoulder and forced her further onto him, his trusts becoming more fevered and fast. She cried out, the pain lacing the pleasure and she shook her head back and forth with braids flying about his outstretched arms.

He cursed, shuddered, and pumped himself twice more before his legs gave out and he sunk back to the floor, her knees once again placed on the cushions. She collapsed on his chest, her breathing ragged and she could hear his heart racing in his chest as a welling frustration burned up inside her.

Banished Gods, you torture me even in my victory.

They lay a while, the heat passing and then rising again, Vanguard taking his pleasure as he would, until her legs were weak and her loins ached. At last he fell asleep, his breathing steady and she rolled off him, the exhaustion taking her away in a shroud of deep slumber.

CHAPTER SIX

SHAY

I have begun to question men, to wonder where their priority lies, although that is ever foolish because certainly it is with them and them alone. Or perhaps, if I think hard on the subject, they are as uneducated as I was not long ago, although even if they weren't I'd have to wonder if they would treat a woman any better.

Nonetheless, I have survived, or so it is my hope. The Sanctuary did not hold my doom but instead my salvation, and I will not forget the blessings received there. Now I must secure my victory, and keep one step ahead of the others for there are surely those inside these walls that will not appreciate what I have done except to steal it from me and use it as their own.

Shay was roused by a woman in violet, the chamber empty other than herself, and the tendrils of sleep still clinging to her as she blinked and wiped her eyes.

"It is time," the woman said.

"Time for what?" Shay asked.

"Your shift is done, you must bathe and then you have an audience with Mistress Alanthria."

Shay's eyes opened fully, "What?"

"Mistress Alanthria awaits you in her study, but you must be cleaned before you see her."

Shay nodded and got to her feet, the woman catching her before she could fall back to the cushions as her legs gave out.

"That was some night, Shay. Drink this. It will restore your strength," the woman said.

Shay took a vial from her, drank from the shadowed-green liquid and felt her spark alight and the strength return to her legs.

"Thank you," she said.

The woman nodded and together they departed the room, a back entrance to the Sanctum opening for them when they reached the end of a labyrinthine hall.

They moved quickly, the halls were less crowded and the women who walked them were mostly metallic-hued. Naked again, the women paid her no mind, and she stayed close to the violet dress of her guide until they made it to another bathing chamber, this one smaller and with a near-naked male attendant.

"The Kapa will service you as needed, but remember the mistress awaits so don't delay too long," the woman said before closing the door.

Shay stood a moment, the lovely and well-muscled young man bowing his head next to a steaming pool. He was naked, shaved at the chin, chest, and even his loins, every cut of his body perfectly smooth and inviting. She covered herself, bit her lip, and then withdrew her hands.

"I guess I don't have to worry about what you see of me," she said.

The Kapa watched her, squinted his eyes, and then shook his head with a shrug.

"You're not a Human, huh?" she asked.

He shook his head again, said something in what she'd determined to be Pargas, and then bowed.

She sighed, moved into the water and felt the warmth wash over her. The frustrations from the night before still pulsed beneath the surface of her mind, but she closed her eyes and tried to relax.

You are here for Vanguard, because of Vanguard, and you are a whore. Remember this, and the fact that he saved you last night, so be grateful...

Swimming to the far side of the pool, she reached out for the soap but the Kapa was there. He held the vial of pink liquid, pointed to it, then his hands, and then the water.

She shook her head, "No, I'm fine, I'll just be a moment."

He nodded and handed the soap over. She took it, let the honey-rich liquid drip into her palm and then lathered herself. It tingled on her skin and smelled of a sweet spice. With her mouth watering, she bathed.

The Kapa stood by, and when she was done he provided a thick towel, but she pushed his hands away when he tried to dry her.

"I've got it, thanks," she said.

He bowed and stood against a wall.

So women aren't the only slaves in this house that must act like dogs to their masters…

After she was dry, he provided her a long silk robe with a golden sunburst and a dozen violet moons on it. She slipped it on and went to the door, the woman in violet waiting for her. The woman smelled her, fussed with her hair, and then nodded.

"Come. This will have to do," she said.

Shay followed as they journeyed down new halls until she finally recognized the stair to Alanthria's study.

It was my hope I wouldn't be back here so soon, and yet that was before I found out the rules and chose to bend them.

The woman pulled a cord to one side of the huge door, a chime sounding and the all-too-familiar bolt on the far side sounding through the wood.

The portal opened, violet light spilling out into the hall. The administrator took a step back.

Shay closed her eyes, took a breath, and then crossed the threshold. A moment after her bare feet touched the interior floor the door slammed shut and the bolt sounded again.

"Come forward," Alanthria commanded.

She moved through the opulence of the chamber, the rugs soft beneath her feet and the smell intoxicating as green vapors slithered through the air with a mind of their own.

Alanthria sat behind her desk, a black silk robe draped over her shoulders and her hair plaited with silver butterflies that hung at her temples and grew smaller as they fell back down her braid.

"Have a seat," the mistress offered.

Shay moved forward, a single chair now stationed before the desk and she took it. Alanthria regarded her with green-tinged eyes as she spun a quill in her left hand.

"I thought you were born here?" the mistress asked.

"I was," Shay replied.

"Then what happened yesterday?"

"I took memories from the womb and utilized them in this life," Shay answered.

Alanthria smiled.

"You know Ixis has been here, she said she gave you the idea for what you did yesterday," Alanthria said.

"And you believe if she had such an idea she wouldn't have used it herself?" Shay asked.

Laughing, Alanthria said, "Well put, and I didn't say I believed her, Shay, my little viper."

There was a pause, and Alanthria pulled open a drawer in the desk and placed eleven golden shaded vials on the top.

"Are you good with math?" she asked.

Shay shook her head, "It wasn't my strongest focus of study at the Academy, no."

"It doesn't really matter I suppose, but I wanted you to see this. You see the girls in the Sanctuary need to procure one of these to be elevated to the status of Lady of the East Sanctum, and ten of them will bring you to the status of Lady of the West Sanctum," Alanthria said.

The mistress put a finger on the top of each counting slowly. When she reached eleven she looked up and smiled.

"In the nearly four decades of service, Ixis, a fine student in our ways and certainly driven, has collected nine full vials. Yesterday, on your second day on the Sanctuary floor, you collected eleven."

Shay's spark flared, her cheeks burning.

"I'm sure Ixis told you she lobbied to get you here?" Alanthria asked.

"Yes."

"She'd be correct, although the advice of the Lady of the East isn't something I listen to. Instead it was a note from Ilcanth that brought you to my attention. You see, during the years I've been at this post only three other noble ladies from the Dead Gate have been brought before me. Two were Lungin fodder after a single night, but the other moved on to become a Vix," Alanthria said.

The mistress stood, walked around the desk and then leaned back against it, the folds of her robe opening to expose her long legs.

"I took you in because I knew what education and noble blood were capable of if the mind was strong enough to excel in this atmosphere, but I truly underestimated what that meant."

Alanthria held out a hand.

"Come, I want to show you something."

Shay took the woman's hand that fully enveloped hers. They walked from the room through a golden circle door into a chamber of violet glass. Alanthria waved her hand, the violet fading and golden lamps lighting within. Beyond the frames a perfect view of the Sanctuary floor played out before them, the half-circle directly below. There, dancing for a gang leader, three women in strange dress preened, and the leader clapped and cheered.

"You see that?" Alanthria asked.

"Yes."

"That is a Pargas folk dance, and their dresses Pargas peasant attire. You did that," Alanthria said.

"Have I done something wrong?" Shay asked.

The mistress shook her head, "No, this will pass, all such things do, but what is important is that you were the first to do it. By tomorrow every Lady in this house will have such a dress in her wardrobe, and within a month they will have fallen to disuse, the floor returning to normal as the novelty among the men we serve will have fallen away to their more base desires. However, the vials on my desk will remain."

Alanthria waved her hand and the glass turned violet once more, the woman sighing.

"For over a century Vanguard sat in that half-circle, as a leader, and another hundred before that as an enforcer, but he never once took advantage of our services. I knew after the first week he'd be trouble, the way you know ill luck will find you no matter your course. If I had a god, I'd have prayed to her that Vanguard be killed, peeled down to a husk on the streets before he became leader, but of course that didn't happen. Truly driven people never allow that to happen.

"I challenged my ladies to break him, and they tried, oh they tried. But there he sat, 9th Day after 9th Day, and year after year...until last night."

"I did what I had to do," Shay said.

Alanthria turned to her.

"And what was that?"

Don't say it. Keep your lips shut!

But the words came out anyway, "I couldn't be on the floor..."

Fool! She is no friend to you!

A smile crossed Alanthria's lips.

"No, I suppose it's not a fine place to live out your years. I spent two years on that floor myself, and I still remember it like it was yesterday. I would put you on the floor so that you might experience it as well, suffer as all the rest, but rules are rules and I'll not be the one to break them."

Shay let out a breath she didn't realize she was holding.

Alanthria looked at her, shaking her head, "You have avoided one terror, Shay, and I commend you for it, but this is the Burning City and none live kind lives. You are now a Lady of the West Sanctum, and with that comes the most rights a Sanctuary Maiden can attain. But you still must provide vials, and Vanguard won't always be here to save you."

"I know that," Shay said.

"I suppose you do." Alanthria walked back toward the door to her study. "And you do realize that what you accomplished may have helped you avoid the Sanctuary, but by doing so the Sisters who would have taken you to their breasts as true kin will now spurn you?"

"They aren't my concern," Shay said.

Alanthria paused at the door, "No, they aren't, but the path you've chosen is a lonely one."

"I'm not here to make friends, I'm here to gain vials, correct?" Shay asked.

The mistress turned and nodded, whispering, "Indeed, and I think you'll be just fine."

Vanguard lay next to her, sweat covering him and his breath coming in great gasps. Shay ached, her loins still pulsing as she clawed the cushions beneath her and struggled to calm her spark.

No release. I must find a way to correct this. Change the subject, clear your mind, find a useful detail.

"What is it like on the streets?" she asked.

He drew in a great breath, turned over and looked at her, asking, "What?"

She leaned up, brought a hand to his chin and stroked the stubble there. He smelled of oil, blood, and old sweat, the combination turning her nose.

"We made a deal. I am to you as you are to me, and we share this pleasure, but there is more to it than that. I can hear you, my paramour, like any girl tucked in a thatched hut with her husband would after a long day's work."

He kissed her finger, asking, "You are a good woman, no?"

"You've given up a great deal because you believed so, and I wonder why only now you ask the question?" she countered.

Another full vial delivered for this night and the ladies of the house surely saw it.

He fell back, stared at the ceiling and the shadowed mosaics deep in the vault above. She lay on him, her hand playing against the cut muscles of his stomach so unlike the round barrel of her husband.

"The streets are vile. Is that what you want to hear?" he asked.

"I want to hear the truth," she whispered.

"The truth is that I've come here to forget that, or isn't that the purpose of the Apothecary?"

She ran her hand further down, played against the hair there, but didn't go further.

"No, the purpose is the release, both in body *and* mind," she answered.

He laughed, "Releasing what is in my mind will drive you mad."

"Women of your land are tougher than that," she said as she grabbed his manhood.

He was already hard, ever ready, and he groaned as she slid down and kissed along his abdomen.

I've seen them do this. I've just got to get past it, do what I must.

The smell was potent – her own essence mixed with his seed and a week's worth of exertion on the streets – and it gave her a moment's pause. Still, she took a breath and brought him to her lips. He moaned, one of his hands tangling in her hair.

Don't gag. Just close your mind.

She took him inside, the taste sour and harsh, but she licked him clean, stroked him with one hand as she worked the head of the shaft. His spark burned, the heat from him washing over her as her jaw ached and he began to thrust upward, each stroke making him mumble.

Do it, give me what you want and so that I can get what I want...

Tension ran through his body, legs stiffening until he forced her down on him, his hand pressing the back of her head as he cried out. She fought bag a gag as he burst inside her mouth, the release spilling out and she drank it down, her lips holding him steady as she continued to slowly stroke the base of the shaft until he relaxed.

It's nothing. Just forget the taste and don't cry. Whatever you do don't cry.

At last he released her head and she pulled away, tucking a stray lock of her hair behind her ear.

"I can only be what you let me be," she whispered.

"Gods... what do you want? Ask anything and I will grant it," he asked breathless.

"I want to know everything the city has to offer outside these doors," she answered.

"Trust me, you don't want to leave these doors," he said.

She nodded, lay back against his chest and rested there until he began to snore lightly.

I've breached the subject now and next 9th day I will push a bit more. All I have is time, time to survive until Colin comes for Caroline, assuming that day ever arrives. Will you stay with me during the countless days? I can only wonder, but now, in this moment, Shay lives and she will prosper and do what is needed, of that too I will make a solemn promise. I will survive, and I will prosper...

Author Scott Taylor has worked as a writer and editor of both fantasy and science fiction for the past decade and is currently the Director of Publishing for Privateer Press, a blogger for Black Gate Magazine's Website, and the founder of Art of the Genre Publishing. He lives in Ranchos Palos Verdes, California with his wife and son where he does his best to keep his mind in both the real world and the various fantasy ones he forever travels in his line of work.